THE "GOSH AWFUL" Gold Rush MYSTERY

Manufactured in Peachtree City, GA

Published by Gallopade International/Carole Marsh Books. Printed in the United States of America.

Picture Credits: Allison Fortune; Launching Success Learning Store (Bellingham, WA); Chilkoot Trail photo courtesy of Canadian National Archives.

Gallopade International is introducing SAT words that kids need to know in each new book that we publish. The SAT words are bold in the story. Look for this special logo beside each word in the glossary. Happy Learning!

Gallopade is proud to be a member and supporter of these educational organizations and associations:

American Booksellers Association
American Library Association
International Reading Association
National Association for Gifted Children
The National School Supply and Equipment Association
The National Council for the Social Studies
Museum Store Association
Association of Partners for Public Lands
Association of Booksellers for Children

Once upon a time...

Papa said ...
Why don't you set the stories in real locations?
Mystery Girl
That's a great idea! And if I do that, I might as well choose real kids as characters in the stories! But which kids would I pick?
MIMI, PICK ME, PICK ME!
ME, TOO, MIMI, PICK ME, TOO!
Christina
Grant
Pick me!

You two really are characters, that's all I've got to say!
Yes you are! And, of course I choose you! But what should I write about?
National parks!
Scary places!
Famous places!
FUN PLACES!
Disney World!
New York City!
Dracula's Castle
GRAND CANYON

On the *Mystery Girl* airplane ...
I can FLY us anywhere!
Mystery Girl
Or aboard the *Mimi*!
Mimi
Take me to the Forbidden City!
Or by surfboard, rickshaw, motorbike, camel ...
All great ideas! I can put a lot of history, mystery, legend, lore, and laughs in the books! We can use other boys and girls in the books. It will be educational and fun!
Good stuff!

Where will you get the other kids, Mimi?
From my Fan Club! Kids can apply to be characters!
Fan Club
And can you put some cool stuff online? Like a Book Club and a Scavenger Hunt and a Map so we can track our adventures?
Of course!
And can cousins Avery and Ella and Evan and some of our friends be in the books?
Of course!
Can I apply?

And so, Mimi, Papa, Christina, and Grant took off aboard the *Mystery Girl* and America's National Mystery Book Series—where the adventure is real and so are the characters! —was born.

ABOUT THE CHARACTERS

Christina
Yother
Age 10

Grant
Yother
Age 7

Zachary
Morris
Age 9

Alexandra
McBeath
Age 7

The TRAIL of '98
DAWSON CITY
YUKON TERRITORY
UNITED STATES
CANADA
YUKON RIVER
CHILKOOT PASS
TAGISH LAKE
WHITE PASS
DYEA
SKAGWAY
BRITISH COLUMBIA
JUNEAU
ALASKA TERRITORY
CANADA
UNITED STATES
TO SEATTLE
GULF OF ALASKA

1

THE GOLD DOME

Christina was convinced that this was going to be one of the most fun adventures that she had ever been on with her grandmother, Mimi, her grandfather, Papa, little brother, Grant, and a couple of friends that they were picking up to join them on the trip.

At the moment, they were standing around the *Mystery Girl*, Papa's little red and white airplane, on the tarmac at a small airport near Dahlonega, Georgia. Mimi, who spent most of her time writing kid's mystery books, was investigating a very curious mystery of her own. She had inherited–from a total stranger–a gold mine!

"I'm sure that if we make a quick stop in Dahlonega, I can find out something about the Gold Bug," Mimi said. She was eager to get underway. The Gold Bug was the name of the mine she had inherited. She believed that the

Gold Rush museum in Dahlonega might have some information on it. She had to start somewhere. The will had not said where the Gold Bug was located.

"How about a little lunch, first?" pleaded Papa. He was always ready for a bowl of soup at lunchtime, and could always entice Mimi with a promise of unsweetened ice tea with lemon and lots of ice–her favorite.

Christina watched Mimi sway her blond curls back and forth as she thought. She tapped the toe of one of her red high heels. No one hoped more than her grandkids that she would give in–they were starving!

Leg 1: Peachtree City to Dahlonega

They'd gotten a pre-dawn start at Falcon Field in Peachtree City, Georgia. As soon as they'd taken off over the pine forests, Papa warned them to "Watch closely!"

They couldn't imagine what kind of surprise he could have for them this early in the morning up in the dark sky. But in just a moment, the sun broke over the horizon. As they banked left to circle past the city of Atlanta, sunlight struck the dome of the state capitol building. It

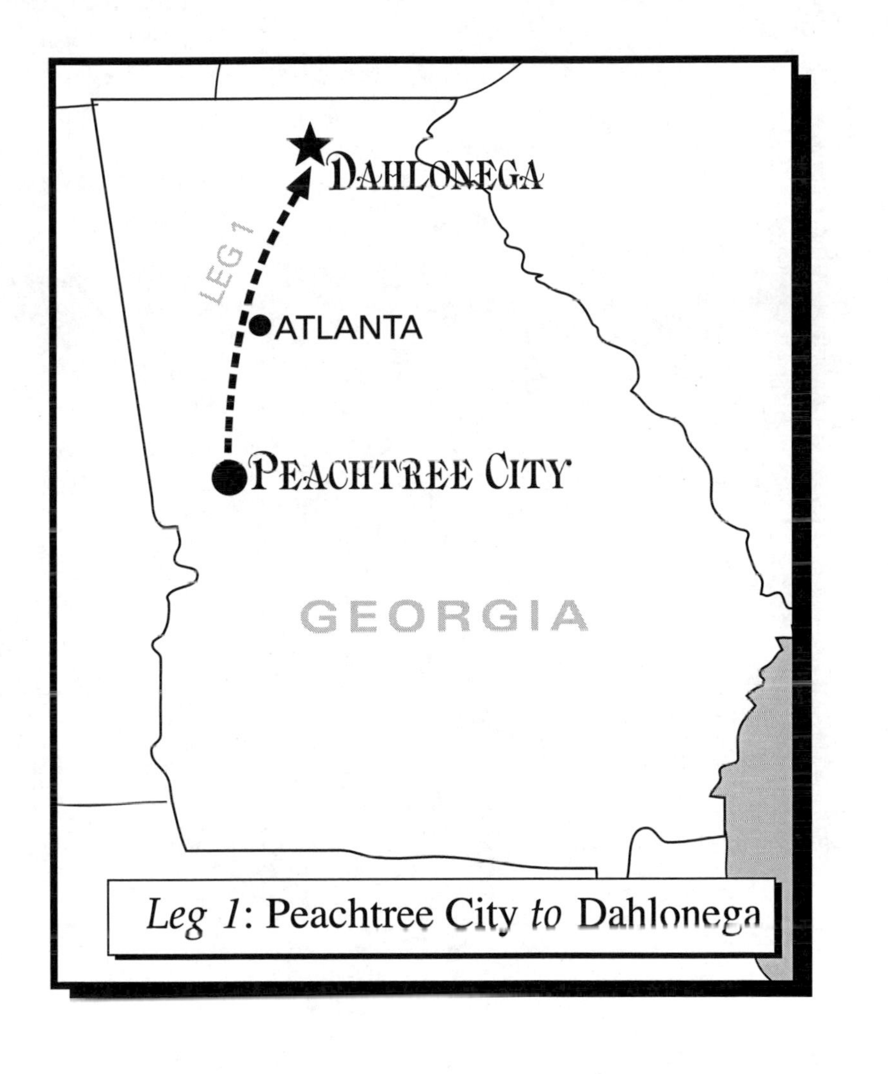
DAHLONEGA
LEG 1
ATLANTA
PEACHTREE CITY
GEORGIA
Leg 1: Peachtree City to Dahlonega

glistened so vividly, that they had to hide their eyes behind their hands.

"You know where all that gold on the dome of the Georgia capitol building came from?" asked Papa.

When the kids yawned and said, "No," he reminded them, "That gold came from a gold rush in our very own state in Dahlonega!"

Mimi looked at the gold watch on her arm, hidden beneath the sleeve of her red suit jacket. "Where we'll be shortly?" she asked hopefully.

"Sooner than those poor folks," said Papa, pointing down to the interstate highway far beneath them, clogged with cars stuck in the morning rush hour.

Grant and Christina yawned again. "Think I'll get in a little nap," said Grant, tugging his jacket up over his shoulders.

But almost before he could nod off, he heard Papa talking to the controllers at the small airport where they were to land. And with one small bounce, they were down, and the adventure had begun.

And, as usual, a mysterious adventure it would be!

2

THE "FIRST" OF MANY GOLD RUSHES

Regarding lunch, Mimi nodded, and Papa led them to a cute café on the quaint town square of Dahlonega, Georgia. The square was busy this sunny Saturday afternoon. The bustling café looked like a giant indoor picnic was in progress with its white tables, checkered tablecloths, yellow daisies in white vases, and families eating and chatting.

They picked a table by the window and ordered homemade pimiento cheese and egg salad sandwiches, chili made with buffalo for Papa, iced tea for Mimi, and big, fat Snickerdoodle cookies for Christina and Grant.

As they waited for the waitress to bring their food, Papa said, "So tell us what you discovered at the museum this morning, and we'll tell you what we bought in a local shop." He gave the kids a wink and they giggled. Clearly, a secret was afoot!

"Yes, Mimi," said Christina, "Tell us again how you came to be the proud new owner of a gold mine!"

Mimi laughed. "It's like I told you," she said, sipping her tea, which had a bright green sprig of mint on top, "a lawyer called me. She said that she was handling the will of a Mr. Jamison Lynn who had died recently of natural causes. He was 104!"

"Wow!" interrupted Grant, "That's older than dirt!"

"Depends on how old the dirt is, buddy," Papa reminded him.

"Let Mimi talk," pleaded Christina. "We want to hear this story."

Mimi smiled at her granddaughter. Christina loved stories–she liked to read them and write them and tell them. "Well, apparently, Mr. Lynn left me the only thing he still owned at the time of his death–a gold mine named the Gold Bug."

Now it was Christina who interrupted. "I've read a story by that name by Edgar Allan Poe. It was really cool; a little scary, but an exciting mystery."

"I always loved that story, too," Mimi agreed. "Edgar Allan Poe was one of my favorites when I was a teenager."

"Excuse us!" said Grant, with a look to his sister. "Back to Mimi's story, please."

"Ok, ok," Mimi said, as the waitress set down their yummy-looking lunches. "The lawyer said that there was little information about the Gold Bug, except that it's somewhere in Alaska."

Papa roared so loud with laughter that the cowboy hat he always wore tipped back on his head. "That helps a whole lot! Somewhere in Alaska, a state made up of a gazillion square miles, most of it frozen!"

"We could get lucky," Christina said with a frown. She really believed that they would find the Gold Bug.

Her grandfather just laughed some more. "That would be a LOT of luck," he said. "You know, depending on luck is how so many folks went bust back during the days of the Gold Rush."

Grant patiently picked the pimiento out of his pimiento cheese. "I'm confused," he said. "If Mr. Lynn was from Georgia, like you told us, then how did he end up owning a gold mine in faraway Alaska?"

"Oh, Grant," said Mimi, "you have to understand more about the Gold Rush." She got a dreamy look in her eyes and they all knew that they were in for a short lecture.

"The Gold Rush was more than just an event, it was a dream, a state of mind," Mimi continued. "Most people lived hard, poor, rough and tumble lives back in the 1800s. They wanted desperately to improve their lives. So when word got out that gold had been discovered in California, it set into motion an amazing chapter of American history!"

"But all that was in California," said Grant. "I still don't understand the Georgia connection."

"Gold's not just found in California," Mimi explained. "There was gold found in Georgia, North Carolina, and other places. Georgia claims the so-called 'first' Gold Rush. But it was California where gold fever struck. People from all over the eastern part of the United States packed up and headed west to seek their fortune, all the way up to Alaska."

Suddenly, Grant got a sort of "gold fever" look in his eyes. "You mean I might find gold right here in Georgia if I dug for it?"

Mimi smiled. "Just maybe," she said. "There are places you can pan for gold around here."

"You might as well buy a lottery ticket," warned Papa, who was a lot bigger on working hard than he was on gambling or waiting for "Lady Luck" to help you out.

But Christina understood that her grandfather was just setting up their surprise. "But you *could* find gold here in Dahlonega, couldn't you, Papa?" she asked with a grin.

Papa grinned back. "Oh, I'm certain that all that glitters is indeed gold here in Dahlonega."

Mimi was suspicious. She looked at Grant, but he just pretended to zip his mouth closed. There was certainly a mystery at their table–and Mimi was the one who was in the dark!

3

ALL THAT GLITTERS...

They couldn't stand it any longer. Papa pulled a small white box with a red ribbon out from under the table and presented it to Mimi.

"Why, what's this?" Mimi asked, truly surprised, which tickled them all, for Mimi was a hard one to surprise. "Because she has eyes in the back of her head," Grant always said.

"Open it! Open it!" the children begged. People at nearby tables overheard the commotion and strained to see what the excitement was all about.

Mimi did not have to be asked twice! She took the box from Papa and blew him a kiss. Slowly, she tugged at the ribbon, stretching out the drama. Finally, she got the box top off, and then fumbled with the red tissue. At last, she revealed the beautiful piece of jewelry inside.

"OHMYGOODNESS!" Mimi squealed, surprised and delighted. "What a lovely necklace! Is this what you all were doing while I was researching–shopping?" She looked at Papa.

"We thought it might bring you luck on this quest," Papa admitted.

"Put it on! Put it on!" the kids squealed together.

Mimi put the necklace around her neck. The gold chain looked pretty against her red jacket. "And what is this thing on the necklace?" she asked, pretending not to know.

"GOLD!" Grant cried. "*Real* gold, Mimi!"

Mimi ran her fingers lightly over the piece of gold and smiled.

"It's a real gold nugget!" said Christina. "It was found in a gold mine right here in Dahlonega! Papa has the papers to prove it."

Mimi hugged and kissed and thanked them all. Nearby guests in the restaurant applauded.

"You know," Mimi said with a smile, "I really do think that this sweet gift from my favorite people will bring me lots and lots and lots of luck."

What neither Mimi, nor her family, could know was that the gold nugget was going to bring them lots and lots and lots of problems—very soon!

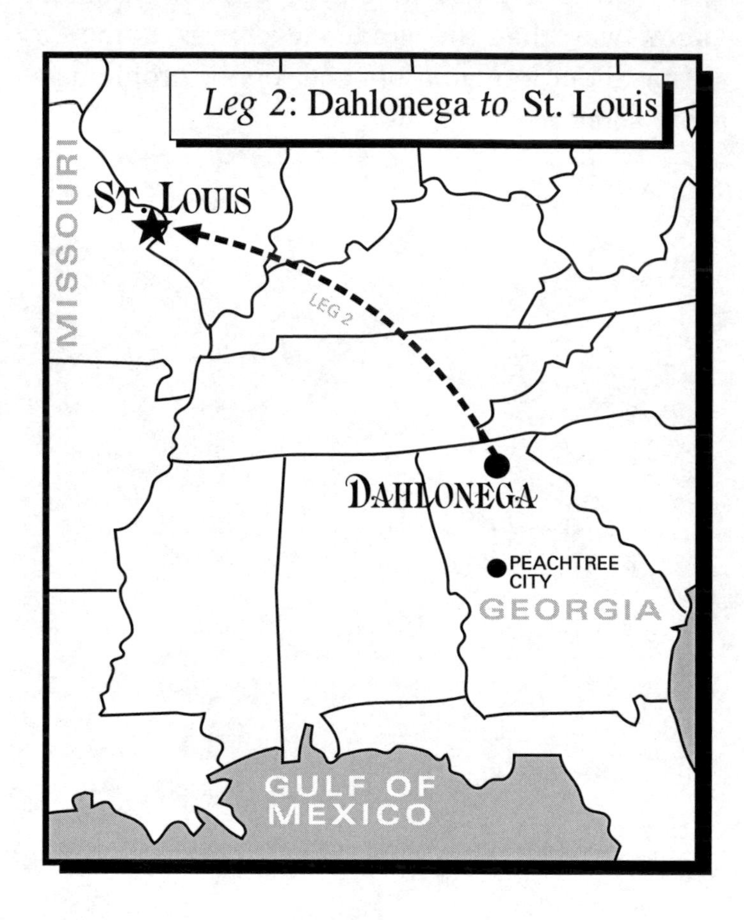
Leg 2: Dahlonega to St. Louis
MISSOURI
ST. LOUIS
LEG 2
DAHLONEGA
PEACHTREE CITY
GEORGIA
GULF OF MEXICO

4

...IS NOT GOLD!

Soon, the family was back aboard the *Mystery Girl*. Papa taxied down the runway and they were soon up, up, and away. In fact, they were on their way to two other small airports to pick up their new friends, Zac, in St. Louis, Missouri, and Alex, in Bellingham, Washington.

Both kids were members of the Carole Marsh Mystery Fan Club and had been chosen to be characters in Mimi's new mystery book for kids–whatever that might be.

"I just never know when or where I'm going to get a great idea," Mimi always said.

Leg 2: Dahlonega to St. Louis

As they flew to their next destination, Mimi told the kids more about the famous period in American history known as the Gold Rush.

"In 1848," she began, "a man named James Marshall was working in Sutter's Mill, California. He spotted a pea-size rock, yellow in color. That rock was gold!"

"Wow!" said Christina, "he must have been excited."

"Oh," Mimi said, "the excitement was just beginning! He was told to keep his discovery a secret, but soon everyone knew that gold had been found at Sutter's Mill. Pretty soon, people made a beeline to California from all across the nation! They had gold fever!"

"What's that?" asked Grant, afraid it might require nasty-tasting medicine.

Papa laughed. "There was such a great desire to find your fortune, that ordinarily conservative, smart, and wise people did some very foolish things."

"Like what?" Christina asked. She knew you could learn as much (maybe more) from people's mistakes as you could from their accomplishments.

Mimi sighed. "Farmers stopped farming. Teachers quit teaching. Sailors jumped ship. Shopkeepers closed stores. Entire families packed up, lock, stock, and barrel, and headed to the gold fields–*certain* that they would strike it rich!"

"And did they?" Grant and Christina both asked eagerly, their eyes wide with anticipation.

"The answer will have to wait till the next leg of our trip," said Papa. "Right now, we're coming in for a landing!"

Zac and his family were waiting for them on the tarmac. They knew that Papa had to keep flying to get to all their destinations before dark. As the plane was refueled, Zac hopped aboard and waved goodbye to his family.

Leg 3: St. Louis *to* Bellingham

"Welcome aboard!" said Papa, hoisting the boy and his backpack up into the plane. "Whatcha got in there–gold?"

Zac laughed. "Sorry," he said. "It's heavy, I know. But I just didn't know what I might need to be a character in a mystery book. What's it about, anyway?" he asked Christina, taking his seat behind her.

"Who knows!" said Christina. "Better buckle up–Papa's ready to take off."

Leg 3: St. Louis to Bellingham

As they sped up into the air and got settled down, Mimi continued her Gold Rush story. "They called all these people who headed to California forty-niners because most of them came in 1849. The next year, California became the 31st state."

"Oh!" said Grant. "Now I remember. We learned that song in school." Grant belted out: "Oh, Susannah, don't you cry for me. I'm going to California with a wash pan on my knee!"

Soon, all the kids were singing the song over and over until Papa raised his "Hush!" hand, and they got quiet.

"Tell us more, please," Zac said.

"Ok," said Mimi. "Then you need to settle back and read a book so Papa can focus on his flying." Papa nodded and Mimi continued, "The forty-niners had the wrong idea. Many of them believed that they could just go out to California and scoop up gold nuggets off the ground! Of course, this was not the **utopia** they hoped for!"

"And to make it worse," added Papa, "people spent what money they had just getting to California. Whether traveling across the continent or by ship all the way around South America, it was expensive and exhausting."

"I saw a picture of that once," said Zac, "in a book. People packed almost everything they owned, then they had to toss stuff out along the way–even useful things like a bed or clothes or pots and pans."

"That's right," said Mimi. "They often went 'bust,' and were in much worse shape and much, much poorer than if they had just stayed home."

"Didn't some of them travel in covered wagons?" Christina asked.

"Prairie schooners!" said Papa. "Sure did!"

"So not everyone made it all the way to California?" asked Grant.

"They sure didn't," said Mimi. "And most of those who did just found hardship, sickness, and even death. Of course, a very few did get rich, but many of those made their fortune providing supplies to the gold seekers, not actually finding gold themselves!"

For a moment, it was quiet as everyone tried to imagine this strange adventure. Finally Christina asked, a serious tone to her voice, "Mimi, maybe we're making a mistake trying to find your Gold Bug mine?

Now Mimi was quiet. At last, she turned and looked at her granddaughter. "You know, Christina, you're right. We are just like those forty-niners–headed off to seek an easy fortune, when maybe we will be disappointed, or only find failure."

"Now, now!" said Papa. "This is just a fun summer vacation trip. If there's a gold mine at the end of our rainbow, good. If not, well, so what?"

"Papa!" said Grant. "There *will* be a gold mine, I just know it. And it will be filled with gold, just like that nugget around Mimi's neck." Grant pointed and they all looked at Mimi's neck.

And looked.

And looked.

But Mimi's brand new gold nugget necklace was gone!

5
BOOM, OR BUST?

"Oh, no!" Mimi cried. "Where is my beautiful necklace?"

It was difficult to look for it on the small, crowded airplane. Mimi checked her clothes, her pockets, and the floor around her.

"Maybe the chain broke," Papa said. "We can search better when we land. Don't be upset, we'll find it."

"Maybe you lost it in the airport," Christina said sadly. "Remember–you did run in to use the restroom while we got refueled."

Mimi looked like she might cry. "Oh, that would be terrible! Someone might find it and return it, but they couldn't they would never know who lost it."

Papa reached over and patted Mimi's hand. "Don't fret. We'll find it, I promise. We'll find your necklace and we'll find the Gold Bug."

Mimi looked doubtful. "I was just off the plane a minute," she recalled. "I think I would have noticed if the chain had broken. That bearded man in coveralls helped me back up the steps right after Zac got on board. So surely, it's on the airplane. Somewhere."

Papa had no more time to worry about the necklace now. "Check your seatbelts," he ordered. "We've been cleared to land, and just in time. There's a storm coming in from the south and it'll be dark soon. I sure hope our ride is here."

They all got quiet. They knew Papa liked quiet when he was landing. The airport looked pretty in the dusky light, the blue runway lights guiding them in. Papa made a smooth landing and they all cheered. All except Mimi, who was very quiet and deep in thought.

As they taxied toward the hangar where the *Mystery Girl* would be parked for the night, they easily spotted the large van waiting for them. People were piling out and waving to them.

"Look!" said Christina, "I'll bet that girl is Alex–our other new mystery book character."

A pretty girl about Christina's age stood patiently with a handful of adults. Christina gave her a shy wave out of the porthole window. The girl beamed and waved back.

As they disembarked the plane, Christina was the first off, and ran up to the girl. "You're Alexandra, right?"

"Yes! Alex," the girl replied. "And you're Christina. I recognize you from your picture in the mystery books. I'm so excited to be included in the next one your grandmother writes. What's it going to be about?"

"Who knows?!" cried Grant.

Alex giggled. "And you must be Grant, the funny character in the book." She put her hand out to Zac. "And you must be Zachary, the other new character. Are you excited, too?"

"Zac," he said, and shook Alex's hand. "Yeah, and we have a mystery already. Ms. Marsh just got a new gold nugget necklace and it's gone missing–right here on the airplane."

The kids all turned to look at the *Mystery Girl* and saw Mimi's and Papa's bottoms as they leaned into the airplane looking for the lost necklace.

"Uh, I guess you'll meet the front of them later," Grant said.

Alex nodded and introduced them all to Barbara Sanford, manager of the Launching

Success teacher store, and her husband. Mrs. Sanford had encouraged her to apply to be a character through the Carole Marsh Mysteries Fan Club. She also introduced her parents. Soon, Mimi and Papa joined them and everyone told Mimi how sorry they were about her lost necklace.

"Lost, or *stolen*," Mimi corrected them.

But there was no time to discuss the matter. They all piled into the van and headed off into the night. Everyone was starving and the kids were especially thrilled when the van pulled up in front of a pretty waterfront restaurant, Alexander's.

As soon as they were seated and had ordered, Mimi explained what was going to happen next.

"In the morning, Papa's going to fly us down to the Sutter's Mill historic site, where we'll pan for gold! Then we have a surprise treat in San Francisco! After that, we head to Seattle to visit the Klondike Gold Rush National Historic Park, and then we head to Alaska to try to find the Gold Bug!"

"Boy, howdy!" said Papa, ever the cowboy pilot, "I'd better eat a ton of this yummy seafood. Sounds like we're in for quite a ride."

Mr. Sanford laughed. "I think I speak for all of us adults when I say I wish we'd applied to be characters in your next mystery, Ms. Marsh."

"So it's going to be about the Gold Rush?" Alex's mother asked.

Mimi shook her blond curls. "Oh, probably not," she said. "I'm usually researching one book while writing another, and editing yet another. We just thought it would be nice for Alex and Zac to come along on this brief summer adventure. Who knows–maybe a Gold Rush mystery would be a good idea?" She looked at the kids who nodded eagerly.

"You know," said Alex's father. "We have some distant relatives who were involved in the Gold Rush."

"They got rich?!" Grant asked eagerly.

The man frowned. "Hardly, young man," he said. "They sent letters home and kept a journal while they were on the Oregon Trail headed to California. They couldn't have had worse luck: they were attacked by a bear, then Indians. They buried two of their group along the trail. Their Conestoga wagon overturned when they tried to cross a raging river. First they burned with thirst in the desert, then they froze and starved in the early winter snow."

"Wow," said Grant, looking sad. "Did they even make it to California?"

Alex's father shook his head. "Only a few, young man, and they were poor and sickly from then on. No strike it rich for them."

"For many," Alex's mother agreed.

When Mimi saw the children looking sad and discouraged, she added, "But we're going to hear some amazing success stories, too!" she promised. "And if you're good travelers, maybe I'll give you some gold from my mine!"

"What?!" all the adults exclaimed.

When Papa explained about the Gold Bug, Mr. Sanford said, "Now, I *really* do wish we were tagging along on your trip!"

"KIDS ONLY!" the children said together.

"Except Mimi, of course," said Christina, who thought her grandmother was really sort of like a big kid.

"And Papa!" said Grant, knowing Papa was just a Big Kid at heart.

"And a good night's sleep," said Mimi.

And after their good night's sleep, Papa got up early and headed to the airport to check the *Mystery Girl* and get her fueled up.

There was only one problem: the *Mystery Girl* was nowhere to be found!

PANNING FOR GOLD

Mimi and Papa were very upset. First, Mimi's gold nugget necklace had gone missing, and now Papa's airplane had vanished into thin air.

"I'm beginning to feel like a forty-niner, myself," groused Mimi. "Our trip to California has been fraught with problems so far. But I think we need to stay on schedule. All the arrangements have been made and people are counting on us."

Papa nodded in agreement. He had filed a police report, and knew nothing else to do for the moment. He had given the officer and the airport manager his cell phone number in case they needed to contact him.

"It's not easy to hide something as big as an airplane," the hangar manager said encouragingly. But Papa knew that anyone could quickly and easily repaint an airplane. He just couldn't figure out how they'd flown it away from the airport with no one noticing.

The kids had stood there a long time now, holding their backpacks, and shuffling from one foot to the other. They figured their vacation was finished, but Christina knew that Mimi and Papa did not give up easily–just like the forty-niners who finally did make it to California.

Soon, Papa had rented another airplane and they were off on...

Leg 4: Bellingham to Sutter's Mill

By the time they got to Sutter's Mill, everyone was in a better mood. They'd stopped at a local diner and had whopper sourdough pancakes. "Just like the forty-niners ate!" a sign proclaimed.

The kids were eager to pan for gold, but first they had to listen to a tour guide, dressed like an old-time miner, give his historic spiel:

"The first forty-niners to reach California were lucky," he said. "Gold was actually pretty easy to find. They could just dig or pan and find gold flakes and nuggets in streams, rivers, or soft

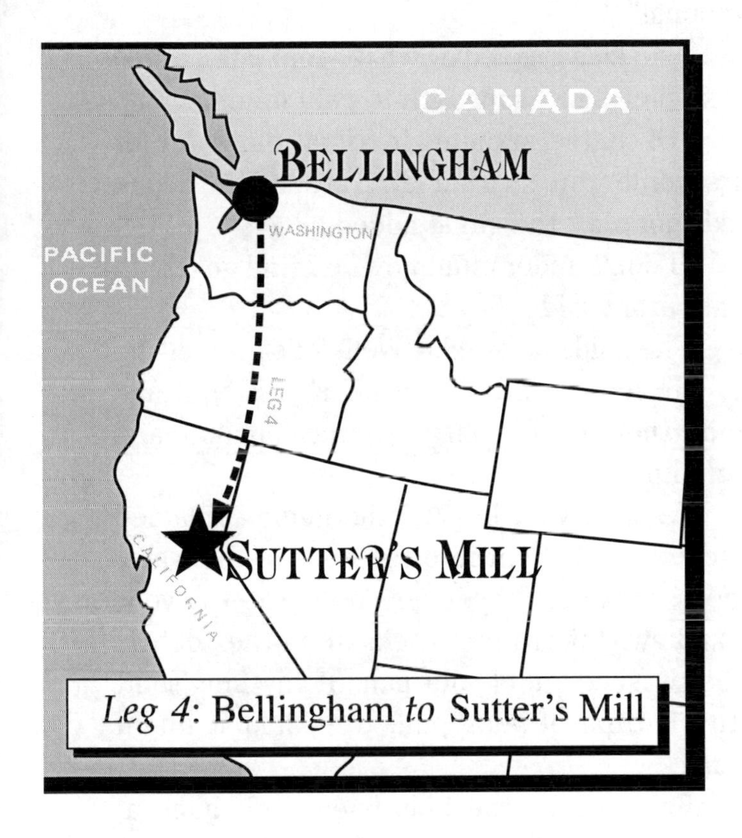

Leg 4: Bellingham *to* Sutter's Mill

dirt. They used whatever tools they had: bowls,shovels, big round pans, knives, forks, or spoons!"

The kids giggled at what Mimi later called the "kitchen sink" approach to gold mining.

"Of course, standing in frigid cold water for hours while you swirled dirt around in a pan quickly got old," the guide added.

"I don't understand how you find gold with a pan," Grant said.

The guide laughed. "Well, let's go see!" he said. He led them off to a nearby stream and handed them each a large, round, shallow and battered pan.

"Gold is very heavy," the guide explained as the kids waded out into the edge of the water in their sneakers. "If you get some water in your pan and swirl it around, rocks and other debris can be swashed out of your pan. If anything's left on the bottom of your pan, well, it just might be gold!"

For a while, the kids tried their hand at panning for gold. At first it was fun, but soon, they became quite discouraged.

"I don't understand what I'm looking for," Christina grumbled, swirling dirt onto her new cargo pants.

"My bottom's wet!" said Grant, "and I haven't seen anything that looks like gold."

Alex tried to be encouraging. "Remember, the guide said some gold looks like corn flakes. Some like peanuts."

"That sounds more like lunch to me," Zac said as he *sloshed sloshed sloshed* the water into and out of his pan.

Grant tossed his pan aside and sat on the creek bank. "I want to find one of those nuggets as big as an apple, like the guide said some forty-niners found."

"I'll take the one the size of a loaf of bread!" said Zac, still sloshing away.

"Well, I want to find a nugget bigger than the biggest chunk ever found...what did the guide say–as big as a pillow?" said Alex.

"It weighed 195 pounds," Christina recalled. "But the gold nugget I'd really like to find is the one on Mimi's missing necklace."

About that time, Mimi and Papa, who had been meeting with the site director, showed up.

"That's sweet, Christina," Mimi said, "but I just want you kids to have fun. My necklace might turn up yet. Things have a way of working out, you know," added Mimi, ever the optimist.

Papa frowned, ever the cynic. "I hope that philosophy applies to missing airplanes, as well," he said. Then he added, "I think I'll try this gold-panning myself, kids. Move over!" And after removing his cowboy boots, with great splashes, Papa grabbed Grant's abandoned pan, and stalked into the water.

"It's a tidal wave!" screeched Grant, reeling back in laughter.

"Well, I don't want to be left out!" said Mimi, who always said she'd be a fourth-grader forever. She slipped off her red sandals, took a pan from a nearby stack, and tiptoed into the chilly water.

"You pan like a girl," teased Papa.

"That could be a good thing," Mimi argued. "I just read that one woman swept her cabin's dirt floor and when she emptied the dustpan, she had more than $500 worth of gold!"

"You always say, 'Cleanliness is next to *goldliness*,'" Christina teased.

"That's not quite how the expression goes," her grandmother reminded her.

The tour guide laughed. "Oh, that cabin floor's not the only strange place gold has been found," he said. "How about cooking a salmon and finding the pan covered with gold? Or digging a grave and finding gold in the hole?"

"Wow!" said Grant, racing back to get another pan. "Maybe I'd better not give up!"

"Trust me," said the guide, sluicing his own pan into the water, "lots of folks who had fought hard to get to California wanted to give up. As soon as the easy-to-find gold was gone, the search for fortune became hard, long, tiring work."

"How's that?" asked Christina, her arms growing more tired by the minute.

The guide said, "Miners found that they had to stake a claim to a certain area in order to have more land and time to hunt for gold. Some used gunpowder to try to blast gold out of the hills. Others used powerful jets of water to try to wash the gold free."

"And when they found gold, were they rich?" asked Alex. She was getting tired, too, and set her pan down to take a break.

"Not usually," said the guide. "Some miners found little, others a tin cup of gold worth about $500, and lucky ones maybe $2,000 worth of gold in a day."

"Sounds like a lot to me," said Zac. He was tired and gave up, too.

"Not when you had to pay your bills," said the guide. "Prices were high. For example, butter was $6.00 a pound; bread, $2.00 a loaf; shoes $50 a pair, and a blanket $100. Eggs could run $5 apiece!"

"Oops," said Christina, "that sounds like the miners stayed broke."

"That's about it," agreed the guide.

Suddenly, Papa roared, "AAAHHHHGGHH! Look what I found!"

Instantly, the kids splashed back into the water and hovered over Papa's pan. In it was a grapefruit-size ball of muck. "Gold!" he said.

The guide grabbed up the ball and splatted it on the bank. "Sorry, mud."

When Papa pretended to cry, the kids knew he had just been teasing them.

Then Mimi, who had been panning patiently, quietly, and in her usual neat and tidy manner, suddenly looked up. There was the gleam of gold fever in her eye! She handed her pan to the guide who took it and peered down into the shallow water. Then he looked up, smiled and winked. He handed the pan back.

"I think you have something here!" he said.

"What? What?!" the kids cried, gathering around,

"Why, gold, of course!" said Mimi. She shifted the pan daintily, just enough for the water to swirl gently. When it did, they all could see the glistening gold flakes clinging to the bottom of the pan.

"Beginner's luck!" said Papa.

"WOW!" said the kids.

"I think I'll pan some more," Grant said eagerly.

"Not now," said Papa. "We have another leg of our trip to make. Time to get out and get dry."

By the time they all had cleaned up and headed back to their rental car, the tour guide caught up with them. He handed Mimi a small vial. "You don't want to forget this!" he said **genially**.

Mimi looked puzzled until she took the vial and held it up to the sun. The gold flecks inside beamed as bright as buried pirate treasure.

"Cool!" said Grant.

"Lucky you, Mimi," said Christina.

"That's a great souvenir," admitted Alex.

"Amazing–real gold!" said Alex.

"In the car, please," said Papa, in the voice he used when he meant, "NOW!"

Digging for gold!

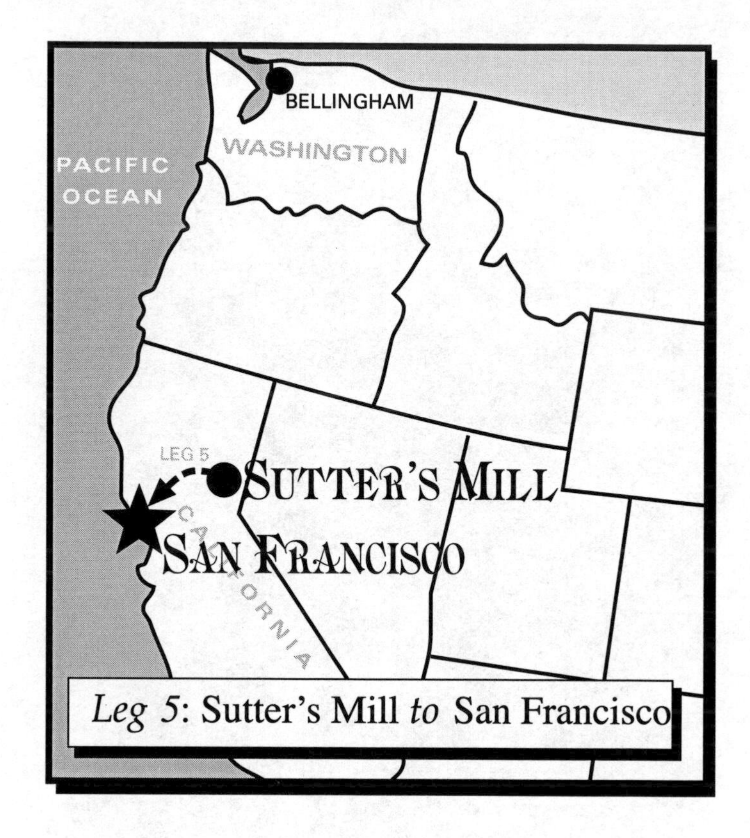
BELLINGHAM
WASHINGTON
PACIFIC
OCEAN
LEG 5
SUTTER'S MILL
SAN FRANCISCO
CALIFORNIA
Leg 5: Sutter's Mill to San Francisco

Leg 5: Sutter's Mill to San Francisco

The kids were thrilled as Papa banked the airplane over the mighty Golden Gate Bridge.

"There's Alcatraz!" cried Zac, pointing to the famous island prison in San Francisco Bay.

The blue water glistened not like gold, but like silver. Whitecaps shimmered in the late afternoon sun. By the time they landed at a small airport across from San Francisco, the city was lighting up like a Broadway show about to begin a performance.

"Why are we coming here?" Christina asked Mimi, who looked tired.

"That's a surprise for morning," Mimi said in a tone that meant, "Don't even try to weasel it out of me!"

Papa was tired, as well. He'd spent hours on his cell phone inquiring about his missing airplane. He'd also checked the Lost and Found at the St. Louis airport for Mimi's necklace. When neither item had been misplaced, mis-parked, or any other reasonable explanation, both Papa and the authorities came to the same conclusion: "Stolen!"

"I'll wait and file a claim when we get back home," he'd told Mimi, who was disappointed and discouraged. She liked to believe the best about people and could not imagine whom, or why, someone would steal either item.

"Just like the forty-niners?" asked Grant, yawning himself. It had been a long day for all of them.

"Well, I meant an *insurance* claim," Papa explained as they taxied to the hangar. "But, yes, the forty-niners did stake their claims, as best they could."

"What's that mean?" asked Alex. "Didn't people honor their claims?"

"Not always," said Mimi, gathering her things. "If an unscrupulous miner got a chance, he became a claim jumper, stealing someone else's land. It was a pretty dog-eat-dog world back then."

"I think I could eat a dog," said Grant, rubbing his empty tummy.

All the kids swore that they were starving.

"Well, give me a minute and we'll be on our way to San Francisco's famous Chinatown!" said Papa, who headed off to get a rental car.

Soon, they were streaking across the amazing Golden Gate Bridge toward the brightly outlined skyscrapers of San Francisco.

Papa never noticed that they were being followed, the bearded driver behind them furiously writing down their license plate number as he drove.

The kids were thrilled to go through the gigantic dragon-like archway entrance to Chinatown.

"This is like being inside a computer game," Grant said. Papa had parked and they were craning their necks to take in all the pink, lime, turquoise blue, and orange neon colors. Red signs with gold Chinese letters announced the name of the many eateries.

Papa was headed toward one special restaurant, The Golden Dragon.

All the kids loved Chinese food. Although the menu was oversized and listed many, many dishes, all the kids ordered their mutual favorite, "Chinese Chicken Nuggets!"

Mimi and Papa ordered more authentic Chinese cuisine. And, as usual, they almost instantly met someone they knew. "One of the nice things about being on the road so much," Mimi always said, "is meeting friends again and again."

The Asian-looking man Mimi had greeted joined them at their table, as the kids unwrapped their chopsticks and practiced using them by tickling one another.

"It's so good to see you, Mr. Mento," Mimi said. "I hope you and your family are well."

Mr. Mento motioned all around the restaurant. "This is my family now, and it keeps me busy."

"We've brought all these little varmints to learn about the Gold Rush," Papa explained. "Perhaps you can tell them how the Chinese fared during that era?"

Mr. Mento looked pleased to be asked and nodded. He turned to the children. "Everyone tried to make a living during the Gold Rush. Here in Chinatown, miners came to buy ducks, fish, fans, pots, or even to get their clothes washed. And, of course, people had to eat." Once more, he waved his arms to indicate his restaurant.

"So, maybe more people made money selling goods and services to the miners than miners made money digging for gold?" Christina asked.

For the first time, Mr. Mento smiled. "Yes," he said, "and tomorrow I hear you will visit a famous emporium that dates back to the days of the Gold Rush." He grinned at Mimi, clearly in on the secret. When the kids looked hopefully at Mimi, she just smiled and shook her head.

When their food came, steaming hot and fragrant, Alex said, "I guess I would have paid a lot for a meal like this after a hard day at the gold mine."

Afterwards, as they strolled to their hotel, they were too tired and too full to bother to look behind them and see the bearded man dodge in and out of alleyways to keep tabs on the family and their friends.

8 A NEW FREE PAIR IF THEY RIP!

The next morning, bright and early, the kids were indeed surprised when Papa pulled the car up to the front of the Levi Strauss Company.

"But we don't need any jeans," Christina said. "You told us to pack anything we would need. Why are we here?"

Mimi laughed. "I just wanted to show you another way someone made money during the Gold Rush–besides from gold."

Papa opened the doors and they all climbed out. "Well, I always need new jeans," he insisted, herding them all inside the enormous store.

As they went in, Mimi said, "Levi Strauss made tents out of canvas. Tents were very important to the miners. But he soon discovered that sturdy work pants that didn't easily wear out were just as important. And so, he invented–JEANS!"

The kids laughed in amazement.

"So now I know why my dad calls his jeans Levi's!" said Zac.

"Mr. Strauss promised miners who bought his Levi's a new pair if they ripped," Mimi explained.

"He never met Grant," said Christina. Her brother frowned, but she just pointed to the rips in the knees of his jeans.

"But Mimi," Christina asked, "how is this helping you find the Gold Bug gold mine you just inherited?"

You would have thought Christina had stated that they were handing out free one hundred dollar bills! Everyone in the store who overheard her remark stopped and turned and stared. Christina blushed and realized that she should probably keep their personal business more private.

Mimi was **curt**. "We'll discuss that in private," she warned Christina.

As her grandmother sashayed down an aisle to help Papa find the right Levi's, Alex asked, "Are you in trouble?"

Christina said, "No. That was just Mimi's way of telling me to hush up. I should have known better."

"Or talked softer," Grant suggested.

Zac took a couple of urgent steps forward. 'Hey!" he said. "I don't think it's you in trouble," he said suddenly. "I think it's your grandmother!"

The kids turned to where he pointed and spied a bearded man who looked like he'd walked right out of one of the gold mines named Bedbug or Fleatown, Chicken Thief Town, or Cut Throat. He was clearly stalking Mimi, but the kids gasped in unison when they saw him snake out his arm and put his hand in her purse!

"Mimi!" Christina cried. "Watch out!"

Confused, her grandmother spun around and slapped the man's hand. Papa rushed forward and grabbed the man by the arm. The store manager, seeing what had happened, ran over to help.

"We do not put up with that kind of thing in our store!" he said sternly to the bearded man. "I am calling the police."

Mimi clutched her purse close to her side. "What are you after, sir? Money? If you need a handout, all you have to do is ask, please."

"Only Mimi could be so nice to a thief," Grant muttered under his breath.

The man hung his head. His watery blue eyes looked as faded as any pair of stonewashed denim jeans in the store. He was slightly dirty, his hair ratted, and his skin wrinkled the way someone's is if they have spent their life outdoors working in the wind and sun.

"Sorry, ma'm," he said softly. "Don't know what I was thinking. Just looking for a handout but hated to ask. Hate charity." His head hung so low, they could not see if his expression was sincere, or that of a fake.

Mimi was not a pushover, but she was a soft touch. She reached into her purse and handed the man a $20 bill. "Get something to eat," she said gently.

Papa and the store manager prepared to argue with Mimi, but the strong-willed woman held up her hand like a STOP sign. "This is the way I prefer to handle the matter, please," she said firmly.

Unhappily, the two men nodded. The miner muttered, "Thank you, ma'am," and without raising his head, quickly walked down the aisle and out of the store. He disappeared around a corner.

The manager looked angry. "Reminds me of the gigantic rats that used to inhabit San Francisco. We had to import cats to get rid of them."

"Anyone can be down on their luck," Mimi reminded them. She turned to shop as if nothing had happened.

"Anyone can be a claim jumper, too," Papa chided her gently.

Mimi just smiled and took the jeans Papa had slung over his arm. She hoisted them up. "And anyone can pick out cool jeans but you!"

The kids giggled. Papa frowned. The store manager shrugged in understanding. And in the alleyway out back of the store, a blue-eyed, bearded face peered through a small window. Although no one saw him, and his expression was impossible to read, he clearly was not done with this family, these friends, and perhaps, not with the theft he most certainly had in mind!

Leg 6: San Francisco *to* Seattle

SEATTLE OR BUST!

Leg 6: San Francisco to Seattle

The children, plus Mimi and Papa, pressed forward on their curious vacation journey. Papa flew them to Seattle, sailing right over Mount Rainier's impressive frosted peak. The Seattle Space Needle poked up into the blue sky.

"Can we go there?" squealed Grant.

Papa laughed. "I thought that's where we'd go for lunch. Mimi's meeting her lawyer there at noon."

The kids cheered as Papa landed the plane. He looked sharp in his new Levi's, his cowboy hat tossed back on his head. He wore a crisp white shirt and a handsome turquoise and silver bolo, a birthday gift from Mimi. His cowboy boots were spit-shined.

Mimi looked sharp today, as well. She wore a new red suit and red heels, but she refused to wear any jewelry until her special gold nugget necklace was found.

It was a good thing that the adults looked good, because as soon as they got off the airplane, they were shocked to be greeted by a handful of newspaper and television reporters, holding microphones and video cameras in their faces.

Papa helped Mimi out of the plane, and Mimi helped the kids, keeping them behind her until they could see what the fuss was all about. Surely, it was a mistake. But it was not.

"Ms. Marsh!" yelled one reporter more loudly than the others. He thrust a microphone in her face. "Tell us about the Gold Bug! Have you located it yet? Is it loaded with gold?"

"Do you know the worth of the Gold Bug?" another reporter screamed. "How did you come to inherit a gold mine?

As other reporters screeched at Mimi, Papa took matters into his own hands, which he raised in the air as he said loudly, "MS. MARSH HAS NO COMMENT AT THIS TIME. NOW PLEASE LET US PASS!"

At Papa's booming command, the crowd of reporters parted, still constantly snapping photographs, and the group walked past them and ducked into a waiting car.

"Sorry for that!" the driver said. It was Mimi's lawyer, Ms. Rogers. "As soon as I saw the headlines this morning, I knew I'd better whisk out here and pick you up." She thrust a newspaper into Mimi's hand and they all read:

DAILY TIMES NEWS

MYSTERY WRITER INHERITS GOLD MINE, BUT FROM WHOM AND WHERE IS IT?

AND, DOES IT STILL YIELD GOLD? SEE PAGE 3...

"Good grief!" said Mimi. "How can this be news and how did the media learn about the gold mine, anyway?"

"The deposition of wills is public notice," the lawyer reminded her. "And anything gold attracts attention in these former Gold Rush parts. And maybe, it's just a slow news day."

"It seems like you have a mystery on your hands, Mimi," Christina said merrily. Secretly, she hoped her picture would be in the paper. It would be great for show-and-tell.

"No thanks, Christina," said Mimi. "This is merely our vacation with a little chore to do, that's all."

"Some chore," said Zac, "finding a lost gold mine."

"I'll bet the reporters pester you until it's found," said Alex.

"Then we should find the mine as fast as we can!" suggested Grant. "This is like a big scavenger hunt, but we don't have any clues. Hard to solve a mystery without clues–right, Mimi?"

Before Mimi could answer, the car pulled up in front of the Seattle Space Needle and they all hopped out.

"Wow!" said Grant, rearing back to look up to the top of the tall tower.

"Inside," said Papa, doing his trail boss job.

Before they knew it, they were riding a glass-walled elevator and oohing and aahing over the city of Seattle spread below, the faint silhouette of Mt. Rainier shimmering in the sky in the distance, and the glistening bodies of blue water all around.

When the door opened, they stepped out into a circular revolving restaurant high in the sky. As they ate, their table would slowly move on the revolving floor until they could see 360 degrees of views.

"We need to talk," said Ms. Rogers to Mimi, as they took their seats.

"Who left Mimi the mine?" Christina asked. "Why didn't they say where it is?"

When the lawyer looked surprised, Mimi laughed. "My granddaughter is a mystery buff," she explained. "And, you know, I'd like to know the answers to those questions myself."

"We all would!" said Alex, and everyone nodded, especially Papa.

"Yes, I would rather not continue on a wild goose chase," he said. "I've got a missing airplane and a gold necklace to track down."

When Ms. Rogers looked surprised, Papa explained.

"Hmmm," said the lawyer. "I know this will sound strange to you, but all this could be connected." She lowered her voice and everyone drew near to hear. "I wanted to meet to give you a copy of this curious will. It appears that the man who left the mine to you knew you somehow. I'm thinking he might have read your children's books. Maybe the *Mystery on the Iditarod Trail*? We believe he may have been a miner once in Alaska, and maybe kept this mine a secret; that's why no one knows where it is."

"But what would that have to do with the thefts of my necklace and our airplane?" Mimi asked.

As the waitress arrived with their lunch, the kids noticed that the adults immediately clammed up.

"This must be some serious mystery," Christina whispered to Alex, who passed the comment on to Zac, who then whispered in Grant's ear.

"This must be thumb silly misty?" he said, looking at his plate. "I thought it was shrimp."

The other kids giggled at how the message had gotten garbled in the passing, just like the kid's game they often played called Telephone.

When the waitress left, the adults continued their conversation. The children ate quietly, all ears.

Ms. Rogers went on in her whisper voice. "To some people," she said, "the Gold Rush is not long ago history, it's like yesterday. There are still unresolved claims, feuds over who got what and when and how. True, that's just to a few people, and some of them are kooks who feel that their forty-niner great-, great-grandfather was claim jumped, or something. If this had never gotten in the news, well, maybe no problem. But anyone who learned about the Gold Bug and thinks it might rightly belong to them, well, they could have been following you or otherwise trying to get more information, in hopes that they could snitch the mine from you."

Mimi looked very worried. "If someone feels that way, then they should get a lawyer and contact me–not follow my family, make me nervous, and possibly start stealing things that certainly do not belong to them."

Ms. Rogers nodded. "I agree. Don't be so alarmed; perhaps I'm wrong about there being any connection, but I felt I had to bring it up. In the meantime," she added with a big smile, "the good news is that one of our researchers found a reference to a Gold Bug in Dawson City. We'd better hurry!"

The kids were so excited that they cheered aloud, causing other diners to look to see what the commotion was all about.

Mimi looked very happy.

Papa said, "As soon as we run our errand here in Seattle, we're Alaska bound!"

Ms. Rogers handed him what little information her researcher had found.

Mimi reached in her purse to get her red lipstick. She looked down and screeched.

"What is it?" asked Grant. "One of those big rats in your purse?"

"Grant!" said Mimi, at the very thought. "No, but something just about as scary. It appears to be a clue!"

Mimi spread a piece of crumpled paper open on the table. In a fat pencil scrawl, almost as if a child had written it, was a warning:

The Gold Bug belongs to me, lady
Stay out of my way
Your fool husband and silly kids, too
Mind your manners, now!

Signed, Long Tom

The lawyer snatched up the note. "Interesting," she said. "Do you have any idea who might have slipped this in your purse?"

"None at all," said Mimi.

But Christina had an idea. "What about that weird man at the jeans store? He was trying to get in your purse before Papa and the manager ran him off."

Mimi raised her eyebrows in thought, but Papa said, "Just a bum, I'd say. More likely trying to snitch a few dollars–which she gave him!"

"He did look like an old-time miner to me," Zac reminded them.

"And he smelled funny," said Grant, squinching up his nose.

"That was probably beer," said Christina with a shudder. "Or some yucky liquor stuff."

Ms. Rogers sighed softly. "Just keep a weather eye," she said.

Grant looked out the window. "But it's a bright sunny day!"

Papa laughed. "She means keep our eyes open for anything or anyone unusual or suspicious," he explained.

"That's Mimi's job," Grant said. And when everyone looked puzzled, he added, "Well, she has eyes in the back of her head, you know!"

After lunch, they said goodbye to Ms. Rogers and headed to the Klondike Gold Rush National Historical Park in Seattle. Mimi felt sure she could learn more about the Gold Bug here, especially since the lawyer seemed convinced that the mine was in that area.

"But I thought the Gold Rush was just in California," said Grant, as they entered the building.

"Not at all," said Papa. "Seattle was a real take-off point to the Yukon for miners in search of Klondike gold."

"This was in the 1890s," Mimi explained. "Gold-finding hopefuls bought supplies here in Seattle, then headed by train or ship up to Alaska and Canada. It was a real stampede!"

As soon as they got their tickets and entered the museum, Mimi said, "I'm going to do some research. Why don't you kids enjoy a tour of the museum? Papa's headed to the bookstore to buy some books for me. We'll meet back here in 45 minutes. Christina, you're in charge."

"No fair!" said Grant. "Why does the big sister always get to be in charge? Next time, I'm going to be born first."

"Get over it, Grant," Christina said. "Why don't you be in charge of leading the way through the exhibit?"

"Ok," said Grant, reluctantly. He squared his shoulders and marched off very officially. The other kids giggled behind his back and he turned and gave them a stern schoolmarm glare.

As they marched on, they did not see the bearded man spying on them through the partially frosted glass windows of the museum.

Right away, Christina and Alex got very excited.

"Look!" Christina said. "I didn't know women and kids went on the Gold Rush!" She pointed to a large photo on the wall of a mother and three young children.

"The girl kept a diary!" Alex said, thumbing through the tattered pages on display.

"That must have been a hard life," said Zac.

"And cold!" said Grant. "Gold in the cold!" He liked to make rhymes.

"Oh, more cold than gold!" said a voice behind them. A man in a park service uniform joined them. "Come on," he said. "I want to show you a special picture downstairs."

The kids followed the ranger down a flight of stairs. There they saw an enlarged black and white photograph mounted on the wall. It was grainy and faded, but the look of unrelenting misery was more than evident.

"Where are they going?" asked Grant.

The kids stared at the single-line string–as far as you could see–of bundled-up people making their way up a steep and narrow and snowy trail.

"That's the Golden Stairs on the Chilkoot Trail," the ranger explained. "It was the gateway to the gold fields in Dawson City, Yukon Territory. There were two ways to get to Dawson City. Those who had enough money traveled by ship to St. Michael, Alaska and then transferred to a riverboat to go up the Yukon River. Others took a ship to Dyea or Skagway, Alaska. Then they hiked over the Chilkoot Trail. From there they would build their own boat to take them down the river to Dawson City."

"It was a struggle," he continued, "just to get supplies to the base of the Chilkoot Trail after the ship dropped them off. People used horses, donkeys, mules, goats, elk, reindeer, oxen, or even dogs to get there. And then the hard part began!"

"The hard part?" asked Alex, wondering what could be more difficult than hauling all you needed to live in a cold environment while hunting for gold.

The ranger laughed. "The miners stacked all their goods at the bottom of the Golden Stairs," he said. "It took most of them 20 to 40 trips to haul at least one ton of goods to the top. It's only one–half of a mile long, but it's a hard climb since it's 1,000 feet steeper from the bottom to the top!"

"Whoa!" said Zac, trying to imagine carrying a ton of goods up such a steep, slippery hill.

"Later," the ranger continued, "some people used White Pass instead. It was eight miles longer, but not quite as steep a climb."

"Boy," said Alex, "I would hate to have two such crummy choices."

The children stared for a long time at the continuous row of ant-tiny people struggling up the steep mountain trail.

"It wasn't a pretty picture," the ranger agreed. "The White Pass route was nicknamed Dead Horse Trail. In the winter of 1897-1898, 3,000 horses starved or froze to death in the snow."

"And where were they headed?" asked Christina.

"To Dawson City," said the ranger. "It was a zoo! Just imagine thousands of prospectors,

Gold-seekers look like ants as they climb the Golden Stairs on the Chilkoot Trail.

merchants, men, women, children, animals, 80 saloons, mud, snow, cold, wind, misery–some folks were so confused they just wandered around, lost, and I'm sure, wondering what in the world they were doing there."

"But I was reading that girl's diary upstairs," Alex said, "and she made it sound like the adventure of a lifetime."

"Oh, it was for many," the ranger agreed. "An adventure–yes. A profitable trip–most often not. Only a few hundred people really struck it rich. The rest went bust. And some folks spent money and time to get there–and they were too late: the Gold Rush was over."

Without thinking, Christina blurted, "Well, I hope not! My grandmother just inherited a gold mine."

"Hmmmm," said the ranger, skeptically. "How interesting. I hope she's not planning on paying your way to college with any gold she might find!" When Christina frowned, he quickly added, "Of course, anything's possible. A secret mine, never mined–now that would be something! Gotta get back to work, kids. Enjoy your tour."

As the kids went back upstairs to meet Mimi and Papa, they still did not spy the suspicious prospector-type peering at them through the frosted-glass window. When he saw the kids, he grinned menacingly. Sunlight glinted off one of his front teeth–it was made of gold!

11

DRY DIGGINGS

"Well, dry diggings," Mimi said, as they left the museum. "I did find one measly reference to Gold Bug and that it was in Dawson City, so that's where we're headed!"

"As long as we don't take Dead Horse Trail!" Grant pleaded with his grandparents.

"I think we'll try something more modern," said Papa. "Like flying!"

Later, when Papa drove up and parked at a dock on the water, the kids were confused.

"This is not the airport," said Grant.

"Sure it is," said Papa, "if you're taking a floatplane!"

The kids were amazed to see that they were going to fly in an airplane with big, banana-shaped floats instead of wheels. "So we can land on the water," Papa explained.

"Cool!" said Zac.

Alex didn't look so sure.

"It's okay," Christina told her. "Papa knows his airplanes. He used to jump out of them when he was in the army."

Now Alex really did look startled. "We aren't going to have to do that, are we?" she asked.

Papa overheard and tousled her hair. "No way," he said. "This bird will land gently on the water–you'll see."

As they boarded the airplane and got settled, Papa's cell phone rang. He stood on the dock and talked. And talked. And talked.

Finally, he hung up and climbed aboard. "Who in the world was that?" asked Mimi, clearly exasperated at the delay.

"The police," said Papa, somberly. "They found the *Mystery Girl*."

Mimi and the kids gasped.

"Abandoned at a grungy little airport on the Alaska/Canada border," Papa said. "The plane's okay, and the authorities are dusting it for prints. I just don't understand why someone would steal my plane," he added sadly.

"It's a mystery," Mimi said.

"Uh, oh, you said the M-word, Mimi,"

Grant teased, but his grandmother ignored him.

"And my necklace?" she asked hopefully.

"No word on that," Papa said with a shake of his head. "I think you'd better give up on them finding that. If someone was going to return it, they probably would have by now, I think." Mimi frowned unhappily, but did not argue with his conclusion.

"Well, let's get underway," said Papa. "Buckle up tight, you kids. We're headed north. Keep thosc warm jackets handy!"

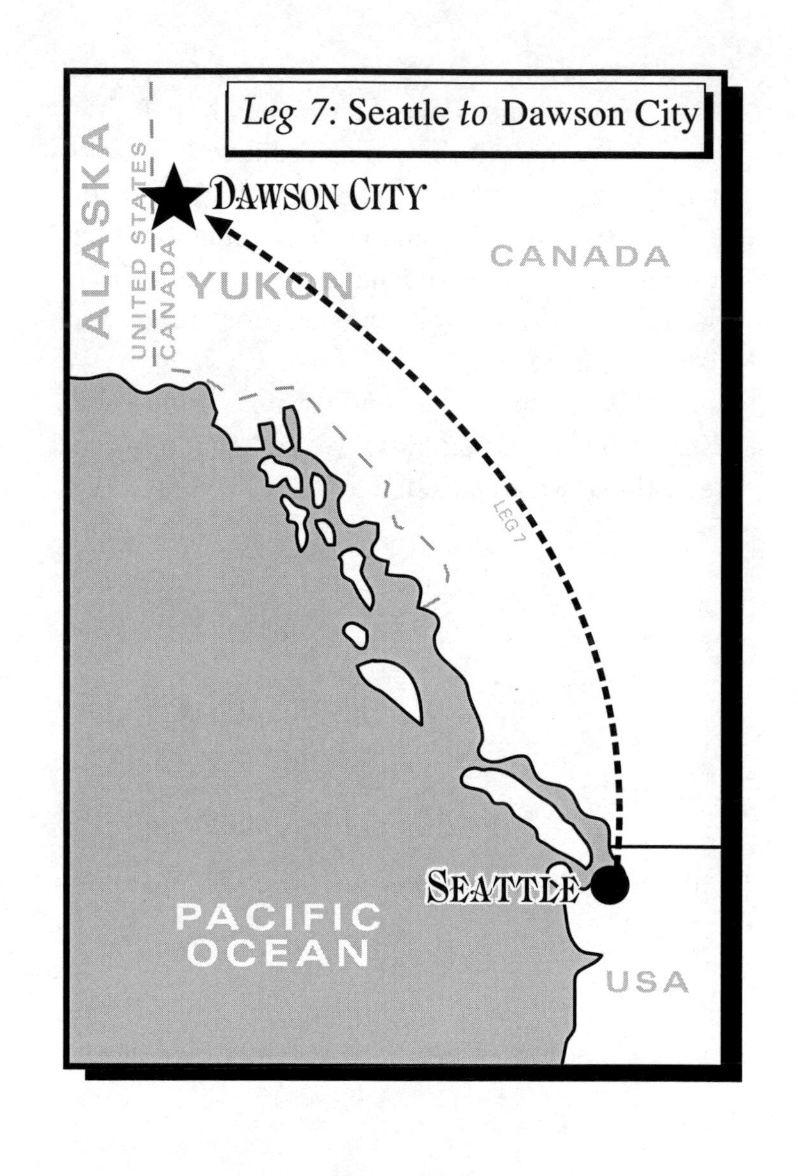
Leg 7: Seattle to Dawson City
ALASKA
UNITED STATES
CANADA
DAWSON CITY
CANADA
YUKON
LEG 7
SEATTLE
PACIFIC
OCEAN
USA

Leg 7: Seattle to Dawson City

The take-off from the water was fun and all the kids looked a little relieved. The flight over Alaska and into Canada was filled with amazing scenery.

"You could sure get lost out here!" Zac said, waving to the immense and seemingly endless array of forest, mountains, and rivers below.

Even though it was mid-summer, the kids put their jackets on long before they landed, and still complained that they were cold.

"Oh, you don't wear those jackets to stay warm up here in the summer," Papa teased. "You wear them to keep the whopper mosquitoes from eating you for lunch!"

The kids giggled, but Mimi tugged her sweater tight. "You'd better be kidding!" she warned Papa, who just turned toward the kids and gave them a big wink.

The landing was as smooth as Papa had promised. The plane bobbed its way to the dock, where two men rushed out to tie the airplane snugly to pilings.

They helped Mimi and the kids out, holding them tightly until they were safely on the dock.

"You don't want to slip through the cracks here," wisecracked Grant, "or you'll get a bath."

"A cold bath, I imagine," said Alex, zipping up her bright green jacket.

One of the men laughed. "Oh, it's hot here right now, young lady." He wore a sleeveless tee shirt and had sweat on his brow.

"Then why do I have an urge to drink hot chocolate?" said Christina. She tugged her jacket's hood up over her head.

"Good idea!" said Mimi. "Let's head to that building over there while Papa settles up. Maybe they have something warm to drink."

Christina looked to where Mimi pointed. The ramshackle building looked as if it had been built in Gold Rush days and not improved upon since. The other kids giggled at the "Leaning Tower of Boards," as Grant called it.

Mimi rapped once on the door and then barged in. "Got anything to drink in here?"

"WHISKEY!" a man behind a counter shouted. When he saw Mimi, he snatched off his fur cap. "Sorry, ma'am," he apologized. "Can I help you?"

"Just looking for something warm for these kids to drink," Mimi said, "but even water will do."

"I can make the kids a Gold Rush cocoa!" he offered. "And you can have your choice of the same or some mighty strong black coffee." He pointed to a woodstove behind him where an old tin coffeepot sat, as well as a softly whistling Williams-Sonoma bright red teakettle!

Mimi smiled as she pointed to the teakettle. The man grinned. As he prepared the cocoa, the kids sat on some rickety chairs around a beat-up table with a checkerboard that looked as if a million games had been played on it, so worn and faded were the squares.

"You the lady lookin' for the Gold Bug?" the man asked cordially.

"How did you know that?!" Mimi asked, her eyes flying wide open.

The man laughed. "Aw, any gold news travels fast up here, ma'am," he said.

"Do you know where the Gold Bug is?" Mimi asked hopefully.

The man came out from behind the counter holding a tray with four big, white mugs. A dollop of whipped cream spiraled up out of each of them. The smell was chocolatey and wonderful.

As he handed each child a mug, they took a cautious sip of the warm beverage.

"Yummy!" said Christina. "This is maybe the best cocoa I ever had!"

"Sure is!" agreed Alex.

Grant just grinned a big whipped cream smile.

"What's the special flavor that makes it taste so good?" asked Zac, taking another big swig.

With a bellow of a laugh, the man said, "Oh, a little gold dust. I put a little gold dust in everything." He gave Mimi a big wink when he set down her mug full of tea.

The kids challenged one another to a game of checkers, while Mimi pulled up a stool next to the man already sitting at the counter.

"You didn't answer my question," Mimi reminded the man. "About the Gold Bug. Do you know where it is?"

The man let out a sigh so big it sounded like the north wind. "Ma'am," he said. "Maybe I do and maybe I don't. But up here we pretty much let folks discover things for themselves. And, you know, I think that is the best bet here all around."

As Mimi stared quizzically at the man and pondered his curious answer, he hopped up off his stool and scooted back behind the counter as the teakettle whined louder.

Just then, Papa barreled through the door. "Had another call," he said. "The *Mystery Girl* is just a few miles from here! What I'd like to do is run over there while we still have daylight and check on her." He looked at Mimi. "Ok? I'll get you a ride into town and be back as soon as possible–by dinnertime, for sure."

Mimi looked dubious. Christina knew she would not like to be in a strange town, not knowing her way around, with four energetic kids to keep tabs on, but she knew that Papa was right about checking on the airplane.

"That's fine," she said. "You go on. I think this nice gentleman will help us find a ride into town. We'll see you tonight." She hopped up and gave Papa a kiss. He grinned and burst back out of the building, leaving the shack quivering as if it might topple.

"I win!" said Grant, slapping a red checker down.

"Good, then," said Mimi. "Let's go. We can get settled in town and Papa will be back soon. We'll find him some good place to eat. He's had a hard day."

Then she turned to the man. "Could you arrange a ride into town for us?"

To their surprise, the formerly pleasant man acted as if he were deaf. When Mimi repeated her question, he still did not acknowledge her, so she hustled the kids out the door and let it slam behind her.

The man who had helped tie-down the airplane offered to give them a ride. Mimi thanked him heartily. But when she turned and saw that he meant in the world's muddiest pick-up truck, she hesitated.

"Not so bad inside," he promised.

Reluctantly, Mimi nodded. "Beggars can't be choosers, I guess!" she whispered to the kids as they all crowded into the cab of the truck.

"This truck has a funny smell," Grant noted as they squished and squashed to make room for everyone. Mimi looked very unhappy to be sitting smack against the driver, who smelled a little funny himself.

"Aw," said the driver, "that's just bear."

"You have a dog named Bear?" asked Alex.

The driver looked at her like she was addled. "No," he said, nice and slow, as if she were not very bright. "I said bear–you know, like does a bear..."

"Umm, we get the picture!" Mimi interrupted. When the kids still looked puzzled, she said, "I think this man traps bears."

The kids gasped and Zac peeked out the back window to make sure that the bed of the pick-up was empty.

The drive was over a bumpy, potholed, rutted road. They all jiggled up and down and scooted left and right on the seat, then jiggled down and up and scooted right and left. The man held tight to the wheel, while the rest of them held on for dear life to one another.

"No seat belts," Zac noted.

The driver frowned. "Where you folks from?"

"Georgia!" Christina said proudly.

"Oh." The man's tone indicated that he didn't think much of folks from "off" as he called it.

Soon, he dumped (that's how Mimi told the tale later) them off at a dump of a hotel, that also appeared to hark back to Gold Rush days. Mimi groaned as they entered the **austere** building.

Christina thought the place looked haunted. She whispered that to Alex, who whispered it to Zac, who whispered it to Grant.

"What?" Grant asked, and the word echoed in the dark, eerie lobby where every bit of wall space was covered with one gigantic animal head or another.

"It's spooky," Christina said.

"Creepy with a capital C," said Zac.

"Are those things real?" Alex asked nervously, staring at an enormous grizzly towering over them in the corner, claws extended many inches and big yellow teeth even further.

"I love this place!" said Grant. "It would be great for hide and seek."

"Hush!" Mimi ordered. In the dim light, she couldn't see very well. Suddenly a sickly, yellowish lamp was turned on at the registration desk.

"Checking in?" an equally sickly, yellowish woman asked, who seemed to have materialized out of nowhere.

"Yes," said Mimi, wanting to add, "Afraid so!"

The clerk shoved a large leather-bound register toward Mimi. When the clerk ran to answer a jangling telephone, Mimi opened the book slowly as brittle, yellow pages crackled.

"My goodness!" she marveled. "This thing must have been used at least a hundred years."

She signed them in and was just about to flip back to the start of the fragile book when the clerk suddenly reappeared.

She thrust a big brass key at Mimi, along with a sealed envelope that had the name of the hotel in one corner–The Dawson City Dead End Hotel. Mimi frowned, but took the envelope and the clerk disappeared instantly, leaving them to find their room for themselves.

"I guess we'll have to carry our own things," Mimi muttered. Just then, the inn's door opened and an ancient, withered, wrinkled, tanned man hunched in and said, "Allow me!" in a chalk-on-chalkboard screechy voice.

"O....K," Mimi said, but she held tight to her purse.

The old man gathered up the kids' backpacks and led them up a rickety staircase to a balcony that overlooked the creepy lobby. He stopped at the end of the hall and grabbed the key from Mimi. ROOM 13 was etched into the wooden door.

"Are you sure you don't have another room?" Mimi asked. She was not superstitious, but still...

"Nope!" the man said with a sneer. "Full up. Always are."

Mimi gave him a disgusted look of disbelief, but handed him a tip, which he frowned at, turned and hunched back down the corridor.

But that was a minor thing. The big problem was when Mimi entered the room first, and...SCREAMED!

Do we have to stay in this spooky hotel?!

12 HOTEL AWFUL!

Room number 13 was one big room with three beds: a large bed and four now-brown brass twin beds. Hanging over the big bed was an enormous moose, his shaggy chin hairs dangling down just over the pillows.

"I cannot sleep under that thing!" Mimi insisted.

"I will!" Grant volunteered. "I think he's cool."

When Mimi called back downstairs, the cranky, old woman insisted that Room 13 was the only room available. Mimi sighed and sat down on the bed, as far away from Mr. Monster Moose, as the kids called it, as possible.

"You kids wash up and put your stuff away. We will go down to dinner while we wait for Papa." Mimi began to set up her ever-present laptop on the small desk. She then pulled out the local phone book from a drawer and looked up Gold Bug.

"Oh, my goodness!" Mimi said to the kids, as they argued over who would sleep where. "The Gold Bug is actually listed in the phone book! I certainly never imagined it would be that easy to find my gold mine. Imagine that! Wait till Papa hears this. We can go see it tomorrow and get out of this gosh awful place."

"When will Papa be here?" Christina asked.

"Any time," Mimi said, checking her watch, "but we will go on to dinner anyway, just in case he runs late."

All of a sudden, they heard a scary sound! It sounded like a moose moan. They all froze and stared at the animal hovering on the wall over the bed. It took a minute for them to realize that the "MMMMRRRRR, MRRRRRRR, MRRRRRRRR!" noise was actually being made by Grant who had crawled under the bed!

"Grant!" Mimi cried. "Get out from under that bed! There are probably dust bunnies under there as old as the Gold Rush and twice as germy. Besides, you almost scared me to death!"

That made Grant laugh out loud, since that had been his plan. When he climbed out from under the bed, dusty indeed, the other kids started a pillow fight–with him as the main target.

Mimi ignored the rowdy children, figuring that they had been cooped up in small airplanes just a little too long. "Cabin fever!" she muttered to herself. She sat at the small desk and ripped open the envelope that the desk clerk had given to her along with the room key. "I can't imagine who sent me a message here," she said to herself. But when she pulled out the scrawled note, a cold chill scooted down her spine.

Christina, seeing the dreadful look on her grandmother's face, tossed her pillow down and asked, "Mimi, what's wrong?"

The other kids stopped pillow swatting and turned to hear her answer. "Just read this," Mimi said. She spread the crinkled note on the desk and the kids hovered over her shoulder and read:

Told you the Gold Bug belongs to me
you should listen or you will see...
things that might scare you,
things that are bad,
if you make me mad, you will be sad.

Signed, Long Tom

"Mimi!" Christina said. "That sounds like a threat. I think you should call the local police right away."

No one noticed that the door to their room had been opened and the quirky bellman stood there grinning. He shocked them all when he announced, "Won't do you any good!"

Mimi turned and glared at the man. "How dare you enter our room without permission!" she said.

The man shrugged. "I knocked but there was a rip-roarin' commotion going on in here. I reckon you couldn't hear me."

Mimi frowned. "Well, what do you want?"

"Sent to tell you dinner's gonna be served right now. Storms a'comin'. Staff wants to head for home early. Better get downstairs if you want to eat."

"What's the big deal over a little rainstorm?" asked Zac.

The man grinned. "No rainstorm, sonny—snow! Big snow storm comin' in."

"Snow?" said Alex, "but it's August!"

"Girly," the man said, "in these parts it snows when it wants to."

"Oh, dear," said Mimi. "I hope Papa gets here ahead of the storm."

"No way," the man insisted.

"And how do you know?" Mimi asked. "How do you know any of our business?"

The man grinned and said. "Ain't you the Gold Bug lady? Everybody in town knows about you."

Mimi did not like the way he made it sound like they were intruders and up to no good. "Please leave," she said. "We will be downstairs in a few minutes."

The man vanished and they all hurried to get ready for dinner, not wanting to go hungry this night, for sure.

"Snow!" Mimi muttered, as they left the room. "What else is going to happen?"

Truly, more than Mimi, or any of them could imagine!

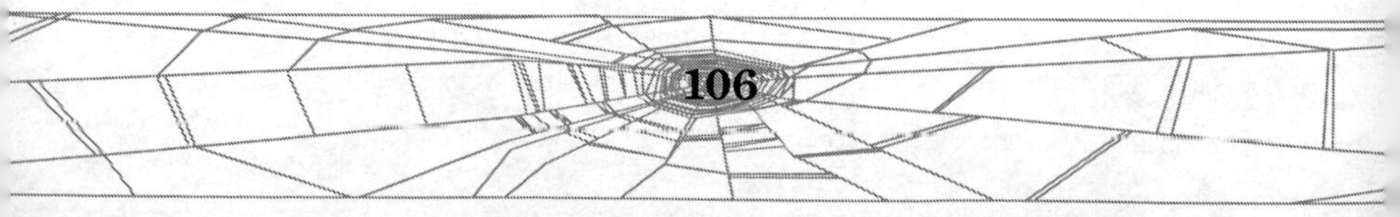

13
A CANDLELIGHT DINNER

When they went down the rickety stairs, they walked into a dining room from the past. It was clear that the diners sat at a large table to eat "family style." Everyone seated at the table stared at Mimi and the kids. They did not speak nor give them any form of recognition or welcome to join them.

"How dangerous can a grandmother and four kids look?" Christina whispered to Alex, who giggled.

"Sit here, children," Mimi ordered, pointing to the five seats at the far end of the table. The girls sat on one side, the boys on the other, and Mimi took the seat at the end of the long table. Two seats remained empty at the far end of the table.

The other diners were all men. Most looked like they were actors in a movie from the Gold Rush era. Their rough clothes, work-beaten hands, and dusty boots made it clear that they were working men.

"Good evening," Mimi said politely as she sat down.

The men ducked their heads and muttered something that sounded more like grunts than "good evening" back to her.

"Put your napkins in your laps, children," Mimi gently ordered, and the kids did as they were told. Surprisingly, the men immediately yanked their napkins from the table and spread them across their dusty pants. Mimi smiled.

As they sat there in silence in the dimly lit room, the hunchbacked bellman and the cranky, old desk clerk began to serve dinner. They came to each guest and slopped something that looked like goop on each oversized tin plate. Bread was passed around, and water poured into yellowed glasses.

Mimi and the kids frowned, but they were starved and each picked up their single fork utensil and tentatively took a taste of the mystery meal. The men were already shoveling food into their mouths.

When Mimi took her first bite, she looked up and smiled. "Why, this is delicious!" she said, clearly surprised.

A few of the men smiled at her. One ventured to say, "Yes, ma'am."

Grant, who never knew a stranger, was intrigued by the men. "Are you guys forty-niners?" he asked eagerly. "Were you here in the Gold Rush? Did you get rich?"

At first, the men froze, then one answered, "Son, the Gold Rush goes on. Ain't the same as before, but there's still mining to be done in these parts."

"Wow!" said Zac. "I guess I thought the Gold Rush was ancient history. I never thought there might still be gold in these hills."

Another man spoke up. "After the Gold Rush, most folks just moseyed home. One man walked all the way back to California pushing a wheelbarrow filled with gold. Some folks sold all their pots, pans, guns, banjos, whatever they had, and used the money to go back home. Some folks just stayed."

Another man appeared eager to talk. "Not the same as before. Now big companies own the mines. Equipment is fancy. Still hard work and a lotta luck–or not–though." The other men nodded.

"Was everyone who stayed behind miners?" Alex asked.

The first man responded. "Nope. Some became teachers, farmers, shopkeepers, builders, loggers, whatever they had done in their former lives. Chinese, Americans, foreigners–we have a real melting pot here."

Christina shyly asked, "And what about the kids who were here back in the Gold Rush? We read about them in the museum in Seattle. What happened to them?"

For a moment there was total silence, then the men began to laugh. Christina blushed. She could not imagine what was so funny.

When the men realized she was embarrassed, one quickly answered. "Why, young lady, those kids–that's us! All grown up. Or at least we're the grandkids of the moms and dads who were forty-niners."

"WOW!" said Grant. "Then you guys are living history! You're famous! Can I have your autographs?"

Now it was the men's turn to blush. Finally one said, "Sure, laddie, soon as dinner's over. We can tell you some tales. Seems like we'll have a lot of time to talk after dinner."

"Why do you say that?" Mimi asked.

The man pointed to the window at the end of the room. They all turned to look and saw that it was snowing. Not just snowing, but snowing hard–a total whiteout.

"Papa!" Christina said, clearly worried and upset.

Mimi chewed her lip. "He'll be along I'm sure," she promised.

Beneath his breath, one of the men mumbled, "Not likely. Not likely tonight."

Just then the door to the hotel screeched open. They all turned to see two newcomers enter the lobby. One was a miner-looking guy with a big beard. The other was a man in a business suit.

When the kids recognized the bearded man, they turned to Mimi with fear in their eyes. "Mimi?" Christina said in a weak voice.

Mimi just looked straight ahead. "Finish your dinner, children," she said softly. But her eyes were not on the bearded miner. She carefully watched the young man in the business suit. He seemed as ill prepared as they were for an August snowstorm and she wondered what his story was. If only it had been Papa who had come in the door. *If only...*

What's for dinner?

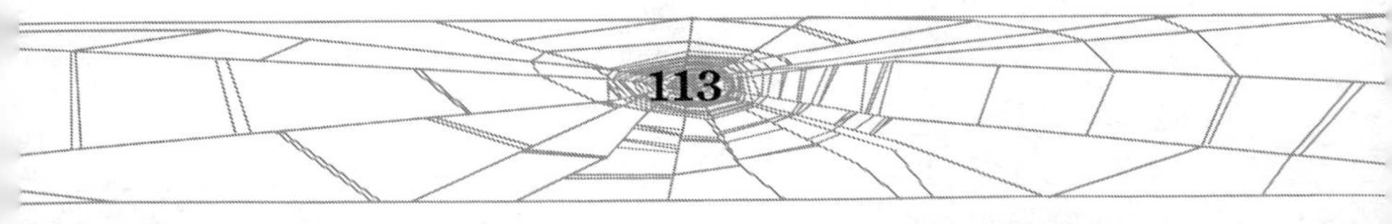

14

SNOW STORM!

As the blizzard raged on, the guests and diners stranded at the hotel tried to make the best of the situation. The two newcomers had not bothered to introduce themselves, but they both seemed to be quite focused on Mimi, and once each of them realized that, they were also focused–and suspicious–of each other. As the two men were served, Mimi, the kids, and almost as if in support, the other men left the table and gathered by the large stone fireplace in the lobby.

To Grant, the unexpected campfire gathering seemed like some kind of lucky Boy Scout outing. He was fascinated by the old-timers, who took to him and enjoyed answering his endless questions, and, yes, signing their names on napkins or pieces of paper.

Christina, Alex, and Zac were more wary of the situation. It seemed that too many bad things had happened already on this trip: the disappearance of Mimi's necklace, the theft of the *Mystery Girl*, the threatening notes, the peculiar people, and now, the freak summer snowstorm.

Mimi was clearly on edge. She had tried to call Papa on her cell phone and now the battery was dead. She kept an eye on the two men at the table, who ate in silence, side by side.

"Ma'am," said one of the miners, politely. "Have you had any long-lost relatives give you a call since you inherited your gold mine?"

It surprised the kids when Mimi laughed. Christina figured that since everyone seemed to know her private business, it did no good to avoid talking about it.

"No," Mimi admitted. "Why do you ask?"

Another of the men chuckled. "Seems like most anyone who inherited a gold mine would discover they had a lot of long-lost friends and relatives!"

Everyone laughed.

"What are the odds an old gold mine still has gold in it?" asked Zac.

"Pretty good," said one of the men, "if it were hidden away and never fully mined."

"Of course," interrupted another man, "it's just as likely you've come on a wild goose chase.

I think most all the mines have been plumb mined out over the years. I wouldn't get your hopes up if I were you, ma'am."

Mimi sighed. "Right now, I have little hope," she said. "In fact, being the proud new owner of a gold mine seems like a big pain in the neck, frankly."

When everyone else opened their mouths to protest, Mimi held up her hand. "I think it's time these children got to bed."

"Noooooo!" the kids groaned together, but in spite of themselves, they each yawned.

Just then a flash of pink lightning and the boom of thunder shook the room.

"What the heck?" said Grant.

"Thundersnow," said one of the men, glancing up from his card game. "Happens sometimes."

"Now, I've heard everything!" said Mimi, looking very unhappy. "Come on, kids, let's get to bed."

As they roused themselves from in front of the fire, a blast of wind shook the hotel...and the power went OUT!

15 SURROUNDED!

The girls squealed. Grant grabbed Mimi's hand. Zac jumped up and tripped over one of the miner's big, dusty boots.

"Stay calm," said Mimi. "It's just a power outage. I'm sure the lights will come back on soon."

In the darkness they heard one miner laugh. "Yeah," he said in a gruff voice. "In about three days!"

In the dark lobby, the flickering embers threw eerie shadows across the walls. The animal heads mounted on the walls seemed larger and more ominous. Even the giant snowflakes threw a confetti of shadows on the wall, making everyone feel disoriented.

"It's worse than a haunted house," Christina whispered to Alex.

Alex whispered to Zac, "Christina says the hotel is haunted!"

When Alex tried to whisper in Grant's ear, Grant pushed him away. "Don't tell me anything I don't want to know!" he insisted.

They all gasped when one of the men turned on a flashlight, which he held beneath his chin so they could see his face. The light turned him into a monstrous sight. Then he lowered the flashlight and handed it to Mimi. "Here," he said. "You can use this to get the kids upstairs. Let us know if you need any help. Some of us have rooms and the rest of us will just camp out here by the fire."

"Just like old times," said another of the men.

Mimi eagerly took the flashlight and thanked the man. They said goodnight, and Mimi rose and told the kids to follow her. When they passed the dining room, they all noticed that the two latecomers were no longer there.

As they climbed the rickety stairs and made their way along the narrow balcony that looked down into the lobby, they were most unhappy to see the bearded miner head into Room 12, and the businessman open the door and enter Room 14.

"Surrounded!" said Christina.

"Shhh!" said Mimi, unlocking the door to Room 13. "Just get your pajamas on and get into bed. It's getting colder in this place all the time." Quickly, the children obeyed. They pulled the thin covers up over themselves in the sagging, little twin beds, and noticed that they could see their frosty breath in the darkness.

Mimi just lay on top of her bed, the moose looming overhead still scary, but not as scary as the situation, the hotel full of curious characters, and the fact that Papa had neither been seen nor heard from. It was going to be a long night!

Will someone please turn on the lights?

16
A MOOSE EXCUSE

In spite of themselves, they all finally fell asleep. The wind continued to roar, the snow to blow, and the temperature to fall. The children dreamed that they were living back during Gold Rush days in a cold, wintry camp with no lights and no warm blankets. There was a lot of tossing and turning and moaning in their sleep.

Sometime after midnight, the door to Room 13 opened. A dark figure entered the room. It went right to the desk and began to fumble through Mimi's purse.

Soon after, another figure entered the open door of the room. In the darkness, it could not see the first man, and bumped into him, turning the desk over with a crash.

Instantly, Mimi was awake! She turned on the flashlight she had held tightly in her hands all night and aimed it across the room. There, the two men pushed and pulled, each trying to gain control over Mimi's red purse.

"STOP!" Mimi screamed.

The kids woke up and stared, wondering if they were still dreaming.

"What is it?" Christina begged her grandmother.

"Who are those men?" asked Zac.

"Make them leave!" pleaded Alex.

Grant hopped out of bed and began to karate kick both the men, who screeched, "Ouch!" and "Stop, kid!" and tried to shove him away.

The other kids hopped out of their beds to help Grant, when the door, which the last man had closed behind him, burst open.

"STOP!" a man's voice boomed so loudly that everyone froze, silhouetted in the flashlight like an old black and white movie.

"Papa!" Christina cried. "Thank goodness you're here! We have thieves! Two of them!"

Just then, the power came back on and they all squinted as their eyes adjusted to the light. In the light, they stared at the two men, each holding a strap of Mimi's purse. Neither would turn loose. The purse was pulled open and the copy of the will from the lawyer stuck out.

As each man grabbed for the envelope, Papa shouted, "DROP IT!"

Neither man obeyed. Both grabbed the envelope at the same time, pulled, and the papers tore in half, each man left with only part of the will.

Suddenly in the hallway, there was a multitude of booming voices that startled everyone!

"You heard the man!" the miners from dinner said. "DROP IT!"

Petrified, the two men stopped and turned. They dropped the purse, but continued to clutch their half of the will.

"Who are you and what are you doing in my room?" demanded Mimi. "You kids get over here with me," she ordered. As they scooted over to her, Grant gave one last karate kick to the shin of the bearded man, who yelped, "Ouch!"

Papa stalked forward, picked up Mimi's purse, and handed it to her. "What is the meaning of this?" he demanded of the bearded miner. "Haven't I seen you before?"

"You have! You have!" the kids cried.

"He's the man in the jeans store!" said Christina.

"Well, it's my gold mine," the man whined. He did not seem dangerous at all, just a wimpy, little man who, perhaps, was not in his right mind.

"What do you mean?" Mimi demanded.

The bearded man looked like he might cry. "My granddaddy mined up here and he always said he'd put a bug in my ear about a place to find lots of gold. When I read this in the paper, I just knew the Gold Bug was mine, all mine." He clutched his part of the torn will to his chest.

"Ma'am," one of the miners interrupted. "This is Long Tom. He's just a local troublemaker, sort of addled. He don't mean no harm. But anytime he hears of a gold mine, he thinks it's his. How about I just take him off downstairs. I'll get him back home in the morning."

Mimi looked uncertain, then nodded. Papa looked unhappy, but also nodded, snatching the half will out of the man's hand as he passed. One of the miners grabbed the man by the arm and hauled him out of the room and downstairs, saying, "Long Tom, you gotta behave now. You're just gonna get in trouble. Haven't we told you and told you..." His voice trailed off in the distance.

Now, all eyes were on the strange businessman.

"And what's your story?" Papa asked, pointing his finger in the man's face. Papa was so angry his hand quivered.

"I have nothing to say," said the man, handing Papa the other half of the will. "I want to call my lawyer."

At this, the miners all began to laugh. "He wants his lawyer," they said in the same tone as when you say someone wants their mommy.

"Ok," Papa agreed. "But you can wait over here until the police come!"

Papa motioned for Mimi to go and sit with the children, then he and the miners escorted the businessman to the big bed where they made him lay down beneath the big moose.

The man looked like he wanted to protest, but realized he was out-numbered by Papa and the miners. Trying to look cool, he stretched out on the bed and put his hands behind his head, as if he were just chilling out. He looked smug. He even had the audacity to smile.

But not for long, for just at that moment...the big, ugly moose fell off the wall and down on top of him!

17

THE GOLD BUG

The next morning, the sun shone brightly and the snow had all but melted. The miners had headed to work early. The police had long ago come and arrested the businessman for trespassing.

No one had slept well, but they had slept a little and were eager to be up, dressed, and eating sourdough flapjacks at the big dining room table.

"Papa," said Christina. "We were so glad to see you last night!"

"I'm like the mailman," said Papa, and when the kids looked confused, he quoted, "Neither rain, nor sleet, nor snow can keep me from my appointed rounds!"

"Not even thundersnow!" added Grant, and they all laughed heartily.

"What's next?" asked Alex. "What about the Gold Bug, Mimi?"

Mimi showed them the telephone directory with its listing for the Gold Bug right on Main Street in downtown Dawson City.

"Seems mighty strange to me," Zac said, "an urban gold mine?"

"Well, it could have been in the middle of nowhere back in Gold Rush days," said Christina. "Maybe the town built up around it?"

"There's only one way to find out!" said Mimi, and they all jumped up and headed for the door.

As they strolled downtown in the sunshine, all the talk was of gold.

"If Mimi strikes it rich, I'm gonna ask her for $5!" said Grant.

"Oh, Grant," said his sister. "That would be nothing. Maybe all that gold could pay our way through college one day."

"Your grandmother will be famous!" said Alex.

"Hey," said Zac. "Maybe she could hire those nice miners to come and work for her. I'll bet they would. Me, too!"

Mimi laughed. "I think we have a little case of gold fever here," she joked.

"Don't you kids count your gold before it hatches," Papa warned. "You've heard of Fool's Gold, right?"

"What's that?" asked Grant.

"Iron pyrite," Papa explained. "It looks like gold, but it's not. Fooled many a miner!"

Suddenly, Mimi stopped cold in the middle of the street they were crossing. The others piled up behind her, almost knocking her down.

"What's wrong, Mimi?" asked Christina. "Are we there?"

The kids looked around for any sign of a mine, not knowing whether that might be a cave-like opening, or one of those ramshackle wooden structures they'd seen at the museum. Instead, what they saw before them was a quaint Victorian–era–looking building, painted pink and purple with beautiful "gingerbread" trim painted white. Over the top of the double door was a sign painted in gold leaf. It said:

"That doesn't look like a mine," said Grant.

"No," said Christina, "it looks like a...like a...bookstore!"

Mimi and Papa began to laugh so hard they had to hold their sides and then each other.

"The Gold Bug's a bookstore?" asked Zac, staring at the cute building with two bay windows filled with books.

"But aren't you upset?" asked Alex. "I mean you thought the Gold Bug was a gold mine!"

"Not at all!" Mimi said. "The will just said Gold Bug," she reminded them. "We just assumed it was a gold mine!"

"Just like Long Tom assumed the mine was his," said Zac.

"And the businessman assumed..." began Christina, who then shrugged her shoulders, "well, I don't know what he assumed."

Just then, a policeman strode up to them. "What he assumed, young lady, is that he could bilk your grandmother out of her inheritance. After we took him into custody last night, we did a background check. He's a talented con artist. And," the police officer looked at Papa, "his fingerprints were found all over the *Mystery Girl*!"

"He didn't know who he was messing with, did he, Papa?" asked Grant, giving his karate pose.

Papa laughed. "No, Grant, he didn't. He finally picked on a family he couldn't outsmart. I guess he'll go to jail now."

"With moose hair up his nose!" said Alex and they all laughed.

Suddenly, they all turned around to see the men from the floatplane launch, the hunchback bellman, the hotel clerk, all the miners, and what looked like half the town gathered behind them.

"What's up?" Papa asked, confused.

"We've been waiting for this day!" the mayor of Dawson City came forward and said. "We've followed the events of your inheritance in the papers. No one had the heart to tell you that it was just a bookstore. We thought it was best that you just came here and discovered it for yourselves. Sorry for all the problems with Long Tom and this other man. I guess you're sorely disappointed?"

Mimi paused in thought, then shook her head and smiled. "Not at all," she insisted yet again. "There's nothing more golden to me than good books and reading!" She looked at the kids to see if they agreed.

"Aw, Mimi," said Grant. "If you say so, I guess."

Everyone laughed and applauded.

The mayor handed Mimi a deed. "The Gold Bug's all yours. Pretty popular store in these parts," he noted. "Lots of reading going on in the cold winter months. I guess you could say," he added, pointing to the store, "that she's a gold mine!"

18
EUREKA!

Mimi sold the Gold Bug on the spot to the mayor. He was ready to retire and to own a bookstore had been his life's dream. "As long as you carry all my mystery books!" she made him promise.

That afternoon they headed out to the local airport where the cleaned-up *Mystery Girl* awaited them.

"I'm sure glad to see her!" Mimi said, giving Papa a big hug. "Just wish I knew what happened to my precious necklace, though."

Papa smiled as he handed Mimi a paper bag. "Eureka!" he said.

The kids gathered around as she opened it. Out came her gold nugget necklace!

"But...but where on earth did you find it?" Mimi asked, near tears.

"The police found it under the plane's seat," Papa said. Then he pointed to some red threads tangled in the chain. "See those? I'm guessing that when you kept looking back at the kids in their seats, the necklace got caught in your suit and pulled off and slid under the seat where we just didn't find it."

"Shoulda used those eyes in the back of your head, Mimi!" said Grant.

Papa put the necklace around Mimi's neck and hooked it. She stroked the gold nugget and smiled. "I'll **cherish** this forever!" she said.

As Papa loaded their gear and went through his pre-flight checklist, Christina asked, "But Mimi, who left you the Gold Bug in the first place?"

Mimi shrugged. "Christina, I guess we'll just never know who my secret benefactor was. We know his name, but not why he picked me. I guess that's a mystery we'll never solve. Maybe it was someone who thought Grant needed $5?" She handed Grant a shiny new five-dollar bill. "Or thought you needed a head start on your college education–that's where the money the mayor paid me is going, you know."

Grant and Christina beamed. Mimi then said, "And I think that my two new mystery book characters deserve to be written up in a new book right away." Now, Alex and Zac beamed.

Then Mimi added, "If only I could think of a subject to write about..."

"Mimi!" squealed Christina.

"*Mimi, Mimi, Mimi,*" said Grant, shaking his head.

"Hey, Christina, turn around!" said Alex.

They all did and a newspaper photographer snapped their picture for the next edition of the *Dawson City News*.

"Hey, Christina," said Zac, "you got your wish. You're getting your picture in the paper!"

"Wish?" said Papa, sticking his head up from beneath the *Mystery Girl*. "What wish? I have a wish. I wish you'd all get aboard–it's a looooooong way home!"

Well, that was fun!
Wow, glad we solved that mystery!
Where shall we go next?
EVERYWHERE!
The End

Now...go to

www.carolemarshmysteries.com

and...

- Add this book to your personal Adventure Map Tracker!
- Go on a Scavenger Hunt!
- Take a Pop(corn) Quiz!
- Hear from Mimi, Papa, Christina, and Grant!
- Talk to Christina and Grant!
- Join the Fan Club...and MUCH MORE!

Gold Mining Tools

Most prospectors only had a few tools. Miners usually didn't have much money, and tools bought in a store were very expensive! Here are some typical tools of the trade:

Pick
The pick was used to break up pieces of rock.

Shovel
Miners used round-nosed shovels to move dirt and gravel.

Pan
Prospectors used a pan to separate the gold from the dirt.

Rocker Box or Cradle

Piles of dirt were washed in a rocker box, which was also known as a cradle. After pouring water over the dirt, a miner rocked the cradle back and forth to separate the gold from the dirt.

Sluice Box

A sluice box was a long trough used to wash gold from large amounts of dirt. After the dirt was washed with running water, gold sank to the bottom of the sluice. The gold was trapped there by wooden ridges. A large sluice box was known as a "long tom." It was 12 to 15 feet long.

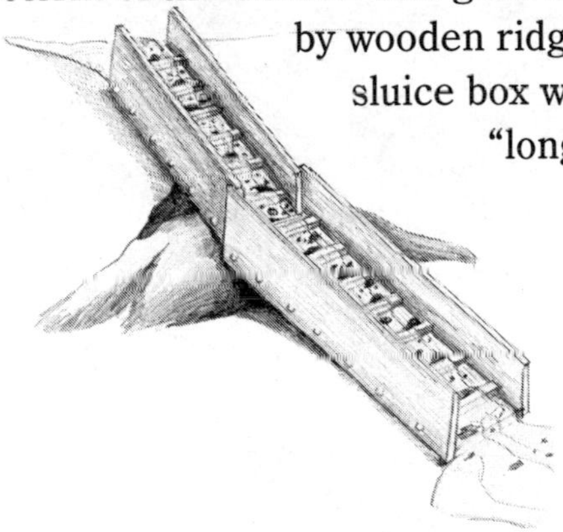

addled: confused thinking

audacity: boldness or daring

bilk: to cheat somebody out of what is due, especially money

Eureka: Greek for "I have found it!"

forty-niner: a miner who took part in the California Gold Rush in 1849

inherit: to receive something from a person when that person dies

long tom: a large, long wooden trough used by miners to separate gold from dirt; the dirt was shoveled into the long tom where running water washed over it

ominous: threatening; like a bad omen

optimist: a person who is cheerful and hopeful, no matter what happens

prospector: a person who searches for deposits of gold or other valuable minerals

thundersnow: a heavy snowstorm with lightning and thunder

SAT GLOSSARY

austere: very simple and plain; not fancy

cherish: to treat with love and care; hold dear

curt: rudely short and abrupt in speech or manner

genial: friendly and cheerful

utopia: an imaginary place of perfection

Enjoy this exciting excerpt from:

THE Counterfeit Constitution

1

WINNER IS?

"Whoooo Hoooo!"

Christina squealed with excitement. Grant hurried into the kitchen to see what all the commotion was about. His sister quickly seized him around the waist.

"What are you doing?" Grant cried.

"It's here! It's here!" Christina swung him around until he thought he might throw up.

"Put me down!" he squealed between breaths.

Christina dropped him abruptly. Grant scrambled to his feet, ready to do battle with his sister, but she had already danced away towards Mimi, who was waving a red, white and blue priority mail envelope.

Rubbing his sore bottom, Grant wandered over to the counter next to his sister and grandmother. "Will anyone who's normal around here please tell me what's going on?" he asked.

Mimi let out a little breath. "A class won my contest! I can't wait to tell you who it is!" She ripped open the envelope. "And the winner is..." While Mimi slid the letter out of the envelope, Christina and Grant jockeyed for position over her shoulder.

"The Fourth Grade class from Elsie Collier Elementary School in Mobile, Alabama!" Mimi shouted. "It says here that they're going to study the U.S. Constitution soon, so we've all been invited to join them on a field trip to Washington, D.C. They've asked me to be a chaperone!"

Christina and Grant gave each other a high-five slap. "Way to go, Mimi!" shouted Grant.

Mimi slid the class picture out of the envelope. "Is that them?" Grant asked. He and Christina looked at all the smiling faces and couldn't help smiling, too. They were going to Washington, D.C.!

"Where's the phone?" Mimi asked. "I'm going to call and accept this invitation right now!" Christina listened to Mimi's side of the conversation. "The National Archives? Of course, that sounds wonderful. As a matter of fact, I need to go there to research my next book! What timing!"

Christina was convinced this was going to be a great adventure! Her grandmother, Mimi, who spent most of her time writing children's mystery books, loved history, and especially loved to visit Washington, D.C. To actually be in the same room with the U.S. Constitution gave Mimi goose bumps.

"Can my pen pal meet us there?" Christina asked. Christina's pen pal Alicia lived in Washington, D.C., and although they had been writing to one another for over a year, they had never met. It would be perfect timing.

"I don't see why not. I'll call Alicia's parents tonight," Mimi said.

By the next morning, everything was set. They would all leave the following weekend, and Alicia and her brother, Mike, would meet them at their hotel in Washington, D.C.

Christina heaved her yellow duffle bag atop the others waiting to be loaded into the belly of the shiny excursion bus parked at the curb of the school. As they waited for the signal to board the bus, Mimi was having second thoughts. Children were everywhere! Some were chasing each other, while others clung desperately to their parents, as this was going to be their first trip without them. Parents were asking last-minute questions, and a woman with a megaphone was barking orders to get the children in order.

Mimi held her hands to her cheeks. "There seems to be hundreds of them!" she exclaimed to Christina.

Their teachers, Mrs. Hudson and Mrs. Whatley, heard Mimi and saw the alarm on her face. Mrs. Hudson had seen it on new chaperones before. As she approached Mimi, she laughed, stuck out her hand, and shook Mimi's with fast, friendly exuberance. "I know things seem a little crazy right now, but things will calm down," she said. "I'm Mrs. Hudson, and we are so excited to have been chosen as the winners of your contest!"

Mimi watched as one of the boys ran by and dangled a gummy worm near Christina's face.

"Stop that this instant, Thatch, or I'll call your parents and have them come and get you!" Mrs. Hudson warned. She patted her brown hair into place.

Mimi's eyes narrowed as any grandmother's would at an unruly child. She wasn't prepared for Mrs. Hudson's reply.

"Spunky little bugger," she laughed, her eyes twinkling. She put her arm through Mimi's and led her to where the bus stood. "Come, I'll introduce you to our principal, Mrs. McRae."

They walked over to a woman with a clipboard cradled in one hand, and a megaphone in the other. She was wearing an Atlanta Braves baseball cap. Mrs. Hudson made the introductions.

"I'm delighted to meet you, Ms. Marsh. I'm a big fan of yours." Principal McRae tucked her clipboard under her arm and shook hands with Mimi. "Later, I want to ask you all about your life as a mystery writer, but for now, duty calls." She jiggled the megaphone. "It's time we get these children loaded on the bus!"

TAWEEEEEET!"

The principal put her lips to a whistle and blew into the bright blue and red megaphone. The children instantly stopped what they were doing. "Okay kids, we're going to take roll call now, just like in class," she instructed them.

"Awwww!" everyone groaned.

The megaphone returned to Mrs. McRae's mouth. "We wouldn't want to leave anyone behind, would we?"

"Nooooooo!!"

They all shouted.

"All right then, let's load 'em up!" her voice boomed. The children hovered around her, anxiously waiting to get started.

Mrs. Hudson, standing alongside Mimi, beamed in happy anticipation. Two boys nearby were talking loudly about the fun they were going to have. "Shhhhh!" She tapped her lips. "Listen, so you hear when Mrs. McRae calls your name."

"As I call your name, please get on the bus," Mrs. McRae said. She wagged her finger at them. "One at a time, mind you."

"Delaney...Brody...Dylan...Jonathan." As Jonathan started to pass her, she stopped him. "Alright, Jonathan, give that frog to your parents. He's not going on the trip with us." "Awwww," Jonathan said as he stepped out of line. He handed the squirming frog to his mother and ran back to the bus. His friends giggled.

"Kendle...Bradley...Jaycie...James... Kellyn...Thatch. And Thatch," she said, giving him a stern look. "I'd better not see those gummy worms in anyone's hair during the bus ride."

"Yes ma'am," he replied, his mouth full of the gooey candy. He gave the other boys a sheepish look as he boarded the bus.

"Kayla...Aiden...Katelynn...Charlie... Alyssa...Megan...Drake...Heather...Oh, and anyone who gets car sick, sit near the front, please," she advised.

On and on it went. A stream of children patiently waited their turn to board the bus as Principal McRae continued to call their names. "Tatum... Tristan... Cartasia... Madelyn...Hollie."

They boarded the bus, each jostling to be first up the steps once their name was called. When Mrs. McRae got to Emily, she paused. "All right, Emily, hand it over." The principal stuck out her hand. Emily reached into her pocket and withdrew a slingshot. "Thank you, Emily," the principal said. "You may board the bus now."

"Devon...Diamond...Kylie...Chris... Hillary...Madison." A tall, gangly boy was next in line. As Principal McRae started to call his name, she noticed that he was standing in front of her in his stocking feet. "Hold it, Gavin. Where are your shoes?" the principal asked. The other kids snickered.

Gavin hung his head. "Dylan threw them on top of the bus!" Everyone turned and looked at Dylan.

"Did not!"

"Did, too!" Gavin shot back.

"Okay, okay!" The back of Principal McRae's neck was beginning to ache, and she rubbed it with her free hand. "Let's get everyone loaded, then we'll send someone to find your shoes," she sighed.

"Joseph...Michaela...Leo...Allison... Abel...Gavin..." Mrs. McRae paused. "Oh dear, two Gavins. Well, we'll just have to watch that." She checked his name off the list. She took a deep breath and continued to call names. "Prika...Tristan...oh, another Tristan...Jeffrey, Andrew, LaFrance, and finally, Autumn," she said with a smile.

The other chaperones boarded the bus last, each shaking Mimi's hand and saying how glad they were to have her join them.

"Well, that's it," Principal McRae remarked, " except for our guest of honor, who's running a little late."

Great, I wish we could just get going, Mimi thought, as she pulled a book to read from her bag.

Suddenly, a hush came over the bus. Mimi looked up just in time to see a familiar, white-haired man trudging up the steps. George Washington had just boarded the bus! As Mimi looked up in surprise, George Washington winked at her and took his seat across the aisle from her.

Thump! BUMP!

The bus lurched away from the curb. They were on their way to Washington, D.C.!